OFF

A.C. McDowell

Cover & Book Design: mycustombookcover.com

Printed in the United States of America

ISBN: 978-0-692-16023-7

First Edition

Dedication

This book is dedicated to three people. My grandmother for introducing me to *Silence of the Lambs*. My mother for allowing me to watch horror movies with her as a child. And to my wife, who not only pushed me to write down my ideas but also sat through countless hours of reading them. I love you all, and this story would not have been created without you.

If not animals, then what are we?

Prologue

A man sits against the edge of a bathtub. The water is close to overflowing. He hears the muffled screams of a man and a woman in the background. But he's not paying attention to that. Right now, he's looking at the dual reflection in the broken mirror that lay shattered on the floor between his feet.

The image.

One of a man smiling, the other of a man with a somber look in his eyes. Tired. *Duality.* A mask and a face. Both staring back at him, wanting to be worn.

The water splashes onto his feet. Cold as ice. The screams become clear as his mind focuses on his victims. He stands up. The reflection becomes one. Light reflects off of the knife in his hand. He exhales as he turns towards the door. Towards the people crawling on the floor, tied and gagged. Towards his new playmates.

"Okay. I'm ready."

Daily Grind

The man laid with his head resting on his pillow, looking up towards the ceiling, counting the seconds until his alarm went off; his little indicator that prompted the start of his day. His morning ritual.

4:00 a.m. Exercise: One-hundred push-ups, One-hundred sit-ups, One-hundred chin-ups. Handstand push-ups until failure. One-mile sprint. Stretch.

5:00 a.m. Breakfast. This usually consists of a peanut butter protein bar and banana oatmeal with chocolate almond milk. His meal is always accompanied by a newspaper.

5:30 a.m. Shower and dress. The news plays in the background.

6:30 a.m. Gather contents for lunch. This is always precisely twenty-six pistachios, forty sunflower seeds, miscellaneous fruit, a sandwich, and cranberry juice. All are separated in their own plastic ziplock bag, with the exception of the juice. He also likes to carry a stainless steel water canteen.

6:45 a.m. Prep and critique

The last part of his morning routine ended with him practicing facial expressions and greetings in the mirror. This was probably the most important part of his daily ritual. And by far, his favorite.

"Hi, how is your day—" *No, too rigid. Try again.*

"Hi, I am—" *No! You're forcing it. Try to make your smile more…natural! Try to look…normal.* He squinted at the strain of it, but succeeded with coming up with something he approved of.

"That will do," he said, finally satisfied.

The man drove to the local shopping center where he worked as a stocker, a mindless job, but one he preferred. It kept him from staring at people for too long by keeping him busy. It kept him from breaking his rules.

He pulled into the parking lot of Smart Shop and parked his car far away from the others. He then checked his face in the mirror. He fixed his glasses, then he smiled a wide grin that slowly transformed into a frown. He stared grimly into his reflection. His eyes were blank, lost somewhere in the emptiness of his existence. He took a deep breath then exited his vehicle. His mask was now on.

He smiled at people as he walked by, giving his coworkers a comforting wave, and greeting customers as they neared. He headed over to the manager's office to clock in. The door cracked open.

"Good morning, David," his manager said in an elated tone.

"Good morning, Michael," the man responded. His manager looked up from his desk to observe him.

"You know, David. I need to know something."

"Yes?"

"Every day, you come in here smiling and happy."

"Yes?"

"What's your secret? I mean, what can I do? To be as happy as you?"

"Practice," the man said with a small grin. His supervisor laughed as if that was the funniest thing he'd ever heard.

"You know, it's funny, because my wife says happiness is a choice, and something you have to work on constantly to have. I guess she's right. But then again, you don't have to live with her every day," his supervisor said, chuckling.

The man just nodded. He didn't have any response to that. And he didn't want to waste time thinking of one. He was eager to get to the stockroom. Eager to start his tasks. Eager to get away from the small talk.

"May I go now?" the man asked sheepishly.

"Yes, of course. Have a good day, David."

"You too, Michael."

The man headed towards the back of the store, walking through a set of double doors. A set of stairs led up to the break room where his locker was held. He went inside and grabbed his apron and tied it on, completing his costume. He was ready.

"What's up, Smiles!" a male voice said mockingly. The man knew the voice. He turned around and faced it.

"Hello, Sean," the man said in a steady tone, filled with nothing. Sean had a devious grin. His eyes went down to the man's hand.

"What you got for lunch today?" Sean asked. The man stared at him. He imagined Sean screaming in pain. He imagined him begging. He wondered what his tears tasted like.

"Are you asking me because you're interested, or because you're going to judge me? You know I bring the same thing in every day. You even made a comment about it yesterday."

"I'm just asking because you carry it in this lunchbox like you're twelve. Your mom make that for you, Smiles?"

"No. My mother is dead," the man said coldly. His face was void of expression, empty. Yet his eyes stared deeply into Sean's and then, the man smiled. "Excuse me. I have to go stock the items now." The man walked around Sean and placed his lunch in the refrigerator.

He exhaled, adjusted his glasses, then headed back down to do his monotonous tasks for the day. He hated his job, but he was good at it. Crushing boxes. Refilling the consumables in the walk-in freezer. Stocking the racks in the aisles. He stayed diligent. His job, however mundane, was a necessary evil. It kept him from doing other things. Things he had sworn not to do anymore.

Before he knew it, the day was halfway over. The timer on his watch went off, indicating his break for lunch. The man walked back up to the break room and spread the contents of his lunchbox onto the table. He sat in the far corner of the room by himself, positioned so he could see everyone that came in. He ate his sandwich, looking—not at the TV, but at the entryway. His mind drifted. He thought about his day.

The people he saw and dealt with.

The rude customers that asked him stupid questions like, "Which aisle is cereal in?" even though they were standing in it.

He thought about how an old lady felt on his butt.

How a younger woman got snippy with him because he

hadn't yet stocked one of the items she wanted. How some people gawked at him like he was an alien. How their eyes judged him and stared like he was a freak. The man thought about killing everybody in the store. How easy it would be to just walk inside the security room and shut the cameras off. How he could lock all the doors and—

The man put his sandwich down. He closed his eyes and exhaled slowly. He took off his glasses and rubbed his temples.

"Are you okay?" a female voice asked from beside him. Her tone was gentle. Concerned.

The man peered over at her. He slowly placed his glasses back on.

"I'm fine," he said plainly, picking his sandwich back up, but not eating.

"I was told that if you drink more water it can help prevent headaches."

"I don't have a headache."

"Oh. Well, what's wrong? You seem stressed," she said, sitting down across from him.

If the man wasn't stressed before, he was now. He craned his neck. Stretching it until it cracked. He looked at her.

"Nothing," the man said with a smile that hurt to fake. He took a bite out of his sandwich, chewing but not tasting. A robotic movement, and as he did it, his eyes stayed on the woman. She repositioned herself uneasily in her chair and looked down.

"I overheard you talking to Sean earlier," she said softly. "I didn't know your mom passed away."

The man stopped chewing. He gave her a glance. He thought her statement was odd. He didn't remember her being in the vicinity during that time, but he wasn't exactly looking for her either.

"It happened a long time ago. When I was young."

"Well, still, I'm sorry to hear that."

The man didn't answer. He just gave her a smile and a nod. She returned the look with an uneasy grin.

"I…I was wondering, you know…if maybe you were free after work…if you know, wanted to hang out?" Her voice was shaky, nervous.

The man kept chewing, his face reactionless.

"Not like a date or anything. Just, you know…me and a few other co-workers are going out tonight to celebrate. It's Mary's sixtieth birthday. If you're free it's—"

"I'm watching someone tonight," the man said tersely. He finished his sandwich and moved on to his small fruits and snacks.

"Oh, you're babysitting?"

"Sure."

"Oh. Okay. I just figured I'd ask. You always keep to yourself. I know how it is when you're new and no one talks to you. I didn't want you to feel like you were excluded."

"I don't feel that way. But thank you. It's very kind," the man replied. The timer on his watch sounded again. He packed up his leftovers and stood up. "Excuse me," he said, walking away. He stopped and looked back towards the woman. "Are you here?" he queried. He had a puzzled look on his face like he was trying to figure something out.

The woman raised her eyebrow. She looked just as confused.

"Excuse me?" she asked with a scoff, letting out an uneasy laugh.

The man shook his head.

"Never mind. You have a cut on your left arm. You should

put something on it."

The woman looked perplexed. She felt her arm and winced at the sting of it. Her fingers came back with small drops of blood.

…

I think sometimes I forget that the world exists within a certain set of rules. Restrictions. Kind of like the ones I set for myself. Only, the world sets rules to keep people safe. I set rules to make sure I'm staying normal.

Safety is an illusion, cast by those in a position of power. The sheep allow the wolves to rule their way of thinking when in actuality, they're only making themselves easy pickings for the ravenous.

We believe in fairy tales. In heroes. Saviors. I've learned there is no such thing as good and evil. Only conflicting morals. Because who's to say one person is good and the other is evil? Take religion, for example. God loves all of his children but only lets the righteous into his house. Meanwhile, the Devil punishes the wicked. Relishing on their torment. In a way, accepting them into his home.

One is a savior. The other is a vigilante. The Bible tells you to fear both. One fear is out of respect and love, while the other is based on a perception of evil. Interesting, I think. How different is God from, say, law enforcement? They judge the wicked, then lock them away for crimes that break the rules of society in a world that teaches you that only God can judge. Should we then consider ourselves Gods? And if that answer is yes, if we are indeed made in God's image, then one must ask: do society's rules apply to us? A conundrum, I know.

But this is what I have found and learned about the actions of people. Most people do not do good because they are good people. They do it because they want to go to heaven. And this is the power of words. The power of those in power. I can control you based on your fears. What a remarkable thing that is…

After Hours

The man left work with a smile on his face, giving peo-ple nods and waves as he headed for his car. And by the time he approached the driver's side door, his face had shifted to something blank and expressionless. He sat in the driver's seat, looking off into the distance, watching as other people left the parking lot. He thought about picking one to follow home. It crossed his mind like a soft whisper brushing against his thoughts.

He closed his eyes and pinched his arm, squeezing into the skin until the pain eased his urges. It was like a crashing wave of peace that flooded everything until silence washed over his thoughts. The man's timer went off again. He slowly opened his eyes and looked down at his watch. It was time for his date.

The man adjusted his glasses, checked his face in the mirror, then drove over to their meeting spot at the park. He sat down on a bench off into the distance, but close enough to where he could see his date as she ran her route. He started eating the rest of his snacks as Amy came strolling down the road.

Across the field and onto her usual trail, like one of God's angels sprinting away with the wind, she wore his favorite outfit: black athletic stretch pants with see-through cutouts, a gray sports bra, and a black baseball cap. Her ponytail hung in the back and bounced with each stride. The man watched her like nothing else mattered in the world. And maybe, for that moment, nothing did.

The man hadn't intended on watching Amy. It just kind of happened. She came into the store one day looking lost. The man observed her as she stood in the aisle biting her lip. Their eyes caught one another and in that brief moment of contact, the man felt everything. Passion, fire, love. An overwhelming burst of desire that sparked between them. And the man was desperate to explore it.

The man remembered how she walked over in his direction, how her hips danced with life and sin. How her skin, so soft and delicate, glistened. And how her voice burned and collapsed his world into ashes. His life, forged a new purpose: her.

The man dreamt of exploring her, but his rules prevented him from touching. *Look, but don't touch*, he reminded himself constantly. It kept him from ruining something good—his progress, and her life. Instead he just watched and observed from afar.

Her small frame and curved hips. Her plump bottom, like a small peach that he imagined biting into. The juice from the forbidden fruit, ripe and bitter with just the right amount of sweetness to taint his taste buds, staining his lips with blood and filling his existence with life.

After Amy's second lap around the park, her gray sports bra darkened with sweat. She was breathing hard. Her breasts bounced up and down as she started to slow. The man could see the imprint of her nipples and turned away—he didn't want to be rude. He stretched his neck to the side until it cracked. He spat the shells of his sunflower seeds onto the ground. Then he watched as Amy stopped. She stretched and left the park. It was almost time for her to get to work.

The man hurried back to his car and pulled out onto the main road as Amy drove by. He made sure he was at least three vehicles away from hers, he followed her back home, and waited as she prepared for work, then proceeded to escort her to her place of business.

Amy worked as a dancer at the local gentlemen's club, where she got paid to take off her clothes. The man wasn't exactly fond of this, but he also knew he couldn't control what his friend did for a living. They weren't exactly serious and he also felt that people should be free to do what they loved.

After Amy was inside, the man headed back home, where he waited for her to finish her shift. He kept his computer monitor on as he ironed his clothes and washed up. He used to follow Amy home back when they first had curious wonderings about each other. He wanted to spend every moment he could to get to know her. But he also realized that in doing so, he was being a bit obsessive. And more importantly, the man didn't want to come off as a stalker. He knew from experience that doing that could be harmful to their relationship.

So now, the man just waited to watch her on his camera feeds that he set up throughout her house. This way he could see her whenever he wanted, and Amy wouldn't even have to worry herself with knowing about it.

He sat down and waited until finally he was notified that one of the motion sensors at Amy's house was tripped. The man's eyes lit up, his heart skipped a beat, his excitement nearly unbearable. The worst part of her working a night shift, was being away from her for so long, while having to sit with the knowledge of what she was doing. Sometimes the man would imagine them living together. Her coming home to see the man with his arms folded. He would imagine the two of them arguing about her working at the gentlemen's club. And after their dispute was over, the man imagined Amy giving him a comforting handshake, one that told him he had nothing to worry about, that he was the only man for her. He then imagined her apologizing to him by accepting her punishment and letting him strap her down to his fun chair. And then, when it was over, he imagined the two of them taking a nice, long bath together as he cleaned off her wounds.

But the man knew that would have to come with time. Moving in together was a big step and he wasn't sure he was ready for that. Instead the man just watched her as she went into her room. And as she undressed, he turned away. It wasn't polite to see her naked. He waited until she got out of the shower and lathered herself with lotion to start watching her again. Amy dressed into a nightie and slipped into her bed, where she pleasured herself. The man didn't turn his head.

He watched as she bit down on her lower lip.

As she squirmed and moaned softly.

As her body shook with soft spasms that washed over her as she climaxed. And as she rolled over and relaxed and turned on her TV. She fell asleep watching her favorite sitcom. And the man watched her for a little while longer as she laid there peacefully. He imagined himself next to her, brushing her hair, kissing her forehead gently while whispering sweet nothings into her ear.

He told her good night. And then, he fell asleep.

...

The darkened night of broken dreams. The river of blood that pours from the lips of corpses rising in the floorboards of a fading realization. That ghosts roam the earth. The mindless cadavers walking aimlessly among the dirt like leeches. They live only to find a host, sucking the world dry.

We live only to feed our own survival.

The dying sun leaves us to shiver and turns us cold like ice among the frozen flames of eternity. We cannot survive here. Lost and damned to this void.

I wonder if the blind can see in the dark.

Is that the only place where they are not lost?

A mind trapped in the fading echoes of a dying consciousness. The wise are on the brink of extinction, fed to the mouths of the entitled.

A hungry beast.

Waiting to take us in.

The souls I have swallowed whole wait for me beyond the gate. It opens. And I walk freely among the tortured spirits.

I am King. I am God. I am everything.

Rise and Shine

The man did not watch Amy in the mornings. His routine didn't allow time for that. He gathered his things and headed to work. When he got there, he checked himself in his car mirror, adjusted his glasses, and smiled. He was ready. He headed over to the office to clock in. And as always, his manager greeted him at the door.

"Davey J! Good morning!" his supervisor yelled. The man just stared at him. "Davey. It's a nickname for David and J because—"

"I know. Because my last name is Johnson," the man said plainly. He kept staring.

"Right. You don't like it?"

"No. I don't. David is fine," the man said, finally breaking eye contact. He had to check himself. Another one of his rules was to never look at a person for prolonged periods of time, even if they were engaged in conversation with him. The eyes were the portals to the soul. And once you look into a man's soul, it's hard not to want to free it.

"Okay, David. No problem. You have a good day."

"You too, Michael."

The man walked towards the back, up the stairs, and into the break room. He saw Sean walking by him, sporting a devilish grin that had an "I'm going to bother you" look written all over it—a daily act that the man was growing tired of. Sean was trying the man's patience, testing him to see how much he could get away with. Sean had no idea how close to the man's limits he actually was. As their paths crossed, the man paid Sean no mind, averting his eyes as he walked by.

Sean grabbed his arm.

The man looked at it with an offensive glare. He turned slowly until he was fully facing Sean. He gave Sean his best, practiced, smile.

"There he is," Sean said, louder than he needed. "Mr. Smiles. Always a happy camper!"

"Hello, Sean. I hope you're having a very good day so far," the man said softly. Oddly, to Sean, it came out sounding like a threat.

"I see you got your lunch all packed up again."

"I do."

"You don't get tired of eating the same thing every day, Smiles?"

"I do believe you've asked me that before, Sean," the man responded, his head tilted slightly, as if he was studying Sean.

"I did?"

"Yes."

"Well, shoot, I must have forgotten, Smiles."

"Does that bother you, Sean?" the man asked with eyes that instantly turned cold. He looked off. Different. His mask broken, allowing a small glimpse at his true face. His aura changed. His presence shifted to something darker. The man became empty and big all at once. Overwhelming. Something primitive broke out in Sean's head, telling him to run. A warning.

"Does what bother me?"

"The fact that I eat the same thing every day. Does it bother you?"

"No," Sean said with a small voice. Almost a whisper. Like a child who was being scolded.

"No?"

"No," Sean repeated, shaking his head. He swallowed hard, his throat was suddenly feeling dry. Sean was scared and he didn't know why.

"Then why do you bring it up every time you see me?" The man's voice was hypnotizing. His eyes were fierce, focused. Sean couldn't break away from his stare. He wanted to, but he couldn't.

"I—"

The man smiled, breaking the tension. His face softened, and everything but his eyes, which held a devious pleasure in them, became friendly.

"I'm just pulling your leg, Sean," the man said, laughing. "You can ask me what I'm eating. I don't mind."

The man moved over to his locker. Sean gave a nervous chuckle. When the man returned, he had his apron on. He placed his lunch inside the refrigerator and lightly patted Sean on his arm. Sean was still standing there, like he was unsure of what to do with himself.

"Let's get to work," the man said.

The man went about his day mindlessly, moving through time without a full sense of it passing. Until his timer went off, indicating his break for lunch. The halfway mark, his day was almost over and it was almost time for him to see Amy. He couldn't wait. He liked to watch her run and stretch and—

"You missed out!" said a woman's voice, breaking the man away from his thoughts. He looked up and saw Kristen sitting down across from him. She had a band-aid on her left arm. The man gave her a look of contempt, but hid it before she noticed. He smiled.

"Missed what?" he said, pretending he didn't know.

"The party," Kristen replied.

"Oh yeah?" the man said with little interest.

"Yeah. It was fun," Kristen said, smiling. The man didn't respond. "You should've came," she followed up. Still nothing. The man just stared at her and chewed, wondering what she would look like without her tongue.

"So, um. How was babysitting last night?" she asked, changing the subject.

"It was fine, I guess."

"Who did you have to babysit? You don't take me as a baby person."

"I wasn't babysitting."

"Oh, you said you were."

"You said I was. I said 'sure,'" the man said, finishing his sandwich. He opened up his bag of nuts.

"Okay. So, you didn't want to come, I take it. You could have just said that; I wouldn't have been offended."

The man thought Kristen was a nice girl, but she was annoying. In different circumstances, he would just make her disappear. He didn't like people noticing him. He didn't like people asking him questions. He didn't like people.

"I know," he said giving Kristen a half smile. "You ask a lot of questions Kristen. You know that?"

"You don't talk much, David. You know that?"

"I don't like talking."

"I see. And all this time I thought you were just shy."

"I'm not."

"I know. I was being sarcastic. Maybe I just like talking to you. Because by talking and asking questions, people who want to get to know you can get to know you."

"Who wants to get to know me?" the man asked, smiling.

Kristen exhaled disappointedly. "Me, silly," she said slapping her hands on the table.

The man watched as her lips scrunched up. Her face annoyed him.

"You want to know what I've learned Kristen? I've learned that if you really want to get to know someone, all you need to do is watch. And listen. A person's body language speaks volumes. Take you for instance. You're about five-foot four, one-hundred and twenty-five pounds. You like onions on your salads and you love the color purple. You have a birthmark on the side of your neck near your ear and you're insecure about it, so you wear your hair to cover it. You eat oat and honey granola bars in the morning with Lactaid milk and sometimes yogurt, but not today."

The man sniffed the air in the space near her face. "No. Today you didn't have any yogurt. You have body image issues because you used to be a little overweight when you were younger. Unfortunately, now that you're slimmer and slightly more attractive, it has caused you to make bad decisions with men. And"—the man said, pointing—"that tattoo on your left arm, the one on your wrist of the butterfly. It's there to cover up the scars you have from cutting. It signifies your rebirth."

Kristen crossed her arms over her chest, her right over her left. She had a disturbed look of shock on her face.

"Would you like me to tell you why you started cutting, Kristen?" the man said, staring at her with an unnerving eagerness.

Kristen sat there silently. She felt naked—violated. Her eyes were wide and red, her mind clouded with things she didn't want to think about. Her teeth started to grind together. Her jaw worked back and forth. She raised her hand, then stuck out her middle finger.

The man's timer went off. He stood up.

"Maybe another time, then. Have a good rest of the day, Kristen."

She didn't respond and the man was glad. He hoped that would stop her from talking to him. At least, maybe, for a little while.

…

I'm obsessed when it comes to information. I love knowing about people, but not because I want to get to know them on a personal basis.

Not always, anyway.

I mostly just like knowing what makes them tick. Digging into their personal lives, finding the moldings of their reality and holding it in the palms of my hands. Searching through it and pulling it apart like a child's toy. Often times I know them better than they know themselves. It's funny, really, how easy it is to figure a person out. Knowing their every move, reading their thoughts without ever hearing them.

I read this quote somewhere and thought it was very profound. It said:

"It is not a problem if I walk into a room and I know everyone, but no one knows me. It is only a problem if I walk into a room and I know no one but everyone knows me." I never go into a situation blind.

Information is power. And the person who holds that power is God.

Off Schedule

The man waited at his usual spot at the park. He kept looking at his watch. He was nervous because Amy never showed up. He waited well until dark, thinking maybe she would show. But to his frustration, she hadn't.

He drove over to her job. She normally worked from 8:00 p.m. to 1:00 a.m. He sat in his vehicle outside of the club, hoping he would see her strolling in. He waited until about 9:00 p.m. then went inside.

The bouncer checked him at the door. The man didn't carry any weapons on him. At least none that would cause suspicion. He'd left his sharp objects inside of his car before walking up. He kept a couple of things on him, though. Modified pens. A handheld flashlight. A pry bar small enough to fit into his pocket. It had a nice little handle that slid over his finger, making it look like a makeshift knuckle-duster.

After an obligatory pat-down by the security guard, the man stepped inside the club. He was assaulted with a barrage of neon lights.

A smell of must. Desperation. Lust.

A girl danced on a platform. Her breasts jiggled and her red thong was consumed by the crack of her butt cheeks. Dollar bills were being flung at her. The man watched as she paid the action no mind; to him, it was a sign of disrespect. It reminded the man of a time when one of his clients threw some money at him. His client never threw anything again.

The man moved through the crowd of men who had surrounded the dancer. They were screaming obscenities and making rude gestures towards her. The man wondered if this is what Amy had to go through every night. He wondered if he should just kill them all. He made notes of their faces in his mind.

He stood near the bar, next to the back entryway, where he could see the whole place. Amy wasn't in sight. He walked up to the bar and stood there and stared at the bartender, who was cleaning off a cup. The bartender gave him a glance. He was a tall man. Young. Muscular.

"Can I help you?" the bartender asked.

"Yes. I'm looking for Amy," the man said with a casual tone and a face void of expression.

"You gotta speak louder, buddy," the bartender said, pointing to his ear. "I can't hear you."

The man leaned closer. He didn't like raising his voice. He didn't like being in crowds.

"I said I'm looking for Amy. Is she here?"

"No," the bartender said, shaking his head.

"No?"

"No." The bartender looked away as he said it, a quick glance to the side. One that the man couldn't help but notice. The intricacies of the human expression was something the man spent countless hours studying. The bartender was hiding something. "She didn't come in today. She called out sick. Are you a client of hers?"

The man didn't respond. He had his answer. He walked back through the crowd of people and out of the club, back into the night like a ghost. He thought about going to Amy's house but decided against it in an effort to avoid being seen. He didn't make good decisions when he was frustrated. Instead, he went home, hoping he would be able to catch her on the cameras.

Once the man was home, he went through the footage. Amy's house was empty and had been for hours. He paced back and forth, periodically checking his computer screen, still hoping that Amy would come walking through her door. But she didn't, and after a few hours of nothing, his eyes were red and dry. They started to close.

When he opened them again, he was looking down at Amy. She was naked. Her eyes stared up at him with fear and panic. Her face was red from the strain of her holding her breath.

She thrashed around in his bathtub.

Water splashed everywhere.

Her body jerked as she tried to push herself out.

Her hands clasped around his, trying desperately to rip herself free, but the man's grip was too strong. She went for his face, but the man just held her down harder. Squeezing her neck firmer until he felt it snap. He watched her lifeless body float under water. Her eyes looked up at nothing, blank like her soul, her expression frozen in her last moments of terror. Air bubbles escaped her mouth. And then, she screamed.

The man woke up in his bed. His sheets and his pants were wet. He'd had another accident. His alarm was going off. He looked at the time. It was 5:30 a.m. He sat up and picked his laptop up from the floor. He looked at the black screen and refreshed it, bringing the cameras back into view. Amy was still not home.

The Hunt

The man paced from one wall to the next. He couldn't shake the idea that his friend was in pain somewhere. Lost and confused and scared. He thought about what a normal person would do in this situation. Should he call the police?

No.

He couldn't. Calling the police would bring unwanted attention to the man. Questions, documentation, reports. That, and the odds of the police finding Amy was slim. If the man knew anything, it was that missing people were hardly ever found. If he wanted to know where Amy was, he was going to have to do it his way. And that meant he would have to get even more involved than he should. It meant giving up the progress he had made. He punched the wall. There was an audible crack as wood splintered.

"No!" he yelled as he hit the wall again. His fist tightened. His knuckles reddened. His thoughts swarmed and crashed like a violent wave that pushed against the corners of his mind.

"No! No! NO!" He was breathing hard. His eyes darkened as he glared at the computer screen, lost in the unchanging image of Amy's house. The man pinched the inside of his arm. He closed his eyes as he started to hyperventilate. He pinched his arm until his nails broke the skin, he eased his breathing and his thoughts, then sat down and went through the footage, starting from yesterday morning.

He watched as Amy woke up. As she stretched and ate breakfast and washed up and dressed. She left the house around 8:00 a.m. He paused the footage and ran his hand along the computer screen, outlining Amy's body. He thought about their first date and how he followed her through the mall as they went shopping. How innocent and peaceful she'd looked. How beautiful she was, even when she wasn't trying.

The man felt a buzzing in his pocket as his phone started to ring. He also heard a car idling outside of his house. He walked over towards the window and peeked outside as he grabbed his phone. A dark blue vehicle was just sitting there. Its windows were tinted, but for some reason the man knew whoever was inside was looking directly at his house. The man watched it for a moment longer, memorizing the plate. He answered his phone as he moved away from the window.

"Hello," the man said with a rugged voice.

"Hi, yes. David?" his supervisor's voice said on the other line. The man looked at the time on his watch. He was late for work.

"Yes," the man answered in a dry tone. He was trying his best to sound unbothered, but he couldn't shake the hints of frustration that were lingering inside of him. He felt everything slipping, like his world was slowly melting away. There was a fire building in him, one that was ready to scorch the earth in wrath. And he knew that wasn't good for his progress.

"Hi, yes. You're, um, late. Is everything okay? You sound a little—"

"I'm sick," the man said sharply. "I'm going to need some time off. Would that be okay?"

"Yes, of course. Take as much time as you need, David."

"Thank you," the man said blankly.

"No problem. If you need—"

The man hung up. He looked back at his computer screen. He sat down and went over the footage again. It showed nothing new. Except for one thing he found interesting.

Amy was talking to someone on the phone prior to leaving her house. The man didn't know what Amy's day job was, but he did remember that the bartender mentioned something about her having clients. The man wasn't sure what was meant by that, but he did know someone who could tell him. And he figured this same someone would, hopefully, be able to tell him why there was a dark-colored vehicle parked in front of his house. He guessed that maybe it was time to go out and make a new friend.

...

I see you there in all your confidence, walking around like death has no plans for you. You're a beautiful piece of work. A walking portrait of art waiting for someone to come along and appreciate your design. I have peeked inside your chamber of secrets and found all the tools needed to make you turn.

I cannot wait to open you up and see what it is that makes you interesting. I dream about you at night, wondering what kinds of noises you make when you scream. The sweet sounds of agony.

I hope you're not ashamed to plead.

I know you are tough. Most people I come across are, or at least they pretend to be. But even the toughest of people can crumble like sand and waste away when you have them in the palms of your hands. It is only then that they realize how precious life is.

You sit a man down and tell him you're going to start cutting pieces of his loved ones off and he will do almost anything you want. How beautiful is that? To give your life for another? I wonder if you will do the same. I know you will.

I can almost taste your tears, and the death that lingers on them. You should drink more water.

Overheating

Joshua was a bartender at night, but in the morning, he liked to work out. He always went early, when there was hardly anybody around. Too late in the day and the gym started to pick up with bodies.

Joshua liked to finish every workout session with a relaxing sweat session in the sauna. And today was no different. Joshua walked in with his towel tied around his waist and one hanging over his shoulders. He sat with his head down and his eyes closed. His mind started to drift as the heat began to rise and after a short while, he started to feel uncomfortable. He sighed. Stretched his neck. Exhaled, and as he did, his phone started to ring. Joshua's eyes shot open. He looked over at his phone. The caller was unknown, which wasn't unusual. He reached over and answered.

"Hello?"

"Hello, Mr. Norbin," the voice on the other line said. Josh scanned around the empty room.

His face was hot against the phone.

Sweat dripped into his eyes.

Steam blew against his body.

"Who is this?"

"Someone who decides on whether or not you get out of here. I have a few questions for you."

Joshua stood up. He walked over towards the door and tried to open it. He couldn't.

"You can ask me whatever you want face to face!" Joshua snapped. A dark figure appeared on the other side of the steamed window.

"Is this better?"

"Let me out! Now!"

"Sure. I'll even leave some water out here for you. I'm sure you're probably very thirsty. If not now, you will be. Even if you don't know it. Pretty soon, your body will dehydrate and you will pass out. And—"

"I have asthma, man," Joshua pleaded as he started coughing. "I can't be in here for this long. Please!"

"Amy. Where is she?" the man asked calmly.

Joshua tried hard to control his breath. His eyes were stinging. He had a perplexed look on his face. "You're the guy from the other night!" he concluded.

"That I am. I would very much like to know where she is. Or, if possible, what happened to her."

"What are you, some kind of pervert? I told you she called in sick. I don't know where she is."

"I would like to believe you, Joshua. But we both know

that isn't true."

"I don't know! Please! Just let me out and—"

"Is that why you sent that vehicle to follow me home? Because you don't know where she is? Also, I would appreciate it if you didn't call me names, Mr. Norbin. I am not a pervert."

The temperature increased and seemed to be doing so at a steady pace. Joshua's skin was burning, hot to the touch. Steam was emitting off of his skin. He started to feel weak, tired, faint.

"You should hurry, Mr. Norbin. I'm sure it's mighty uncomfortable in there."

"Listen, man. I don't know where she is, okay?"

"You asked if I was her client. Why?"

"Because some of our girls also work as escorts for Mr. Moretti. My boss sometimes gets offers for girls like Amy."

"Girls like her?"

"Yeah. Ones who have no family. No identity. Those girls sometimes get sold. We don't see them anymore after that. New girls come in. That's all I know, I swear!" Joshua was leaning against the wall now. His skin turned red. He was cooking.

"And the van?"

"I don't know anything about that! I called my boss and told him you were asking about Amy. Gave him your description and that's it man, I swear. I'm just the bartender, man, please." Joshua felt like he was going to throw up. He bent over and started dry heaving. His stomach contracted. The air became thick and sharp, like tiny knives that ran down into his lungs, cutting him with each breath.

"One last question. Where can I find your boss, Mr. Moretti?"

"At the club. He's always there. Now please let me out!"

The man didn't respond. He just stood there for a moment watching from the other side of the mirror. He then drew a happy face on it and walked away. Joshua tried the door again but it was still locked. He banged on it weakly. He slumped down and fell to the floor. His vision became blurry. His thoughts became quiet.

Saying Hello

The man went back home and thought hard about what he had just done. He also thought about his next move. He wondered if he should have a next move. Ultimately, he was satisfied with the new information he gathered. In fact, he felt better than he had in months. He felt some sort of accomplishment. Purpose. Although he did feel himself slipping back into his old ways…

He had a rule of not killing anyone…anymore. And although he was sure someone would eventually find Mr. Norbin, he couldn't be sure that the man wouldn't overheat in there and die from exhaustion. He worried that if he broke his rule, even once, even unintentionally, that he would keep on breaking it.

But was that necessarily a bad thing? Someone had Amy somewhere doing something that was painful for the man to imagine. He needed to help her. And if he was going to help her, he needed to know what that would cost him and if it would be worth it. He needed to decide if she was worth his soul, and after a moment's thought, he decided he had no soul. He had no identity. He had no name or memory of a time when any of those things were ever important to him. He did, however, remember all the fun times he had with Amy. Watching her at the park. Watching her pleasure herself at night after her long hot showers. Watching her sleep and looking at her beautiful smile when she watched television. He made up his mind. He decided he would—

A notification appeared on his computer screen. His stomach dropped at the sight of it. He hurried over and opened up his camera views, and his face scrunched up with disappointment. The motion sensors were tripped. But not by Amy. Inside the house was a man in dark clothing. It looked like he was going through the house. It looked like he was looking through Amy's things.

The man's fist tightened.

He stood up and stretched his neck to the side, cracking it. He grabbed his jacket. A hat. Some disposable gloves and headed out the door. He needed to see the intruder up close. He needed to talk to him about going through people's things without their permission.

He drove over to Amy's house, parking far away from it. He walked around the block and saw a four-door sedan idling outside of Amy's home. There was a man sitting in the driver's seat. He looked pretty distracted as he periodically checked his watch and glanced over towards the house. Otherwise he was looking at his phone, which made it easy for the man to walk up towards the side of the vehicle unnoticed.

The man stood near the car window, watching the driver as he remained oblivious to his presence. After a moment of being unnoticed, the man knocked on the window, causing the driver to jump and also alerting him to the man's presence. One of his hands went to his waistband as he rolled down the window.

"Excuse me. Can you tell me—"

"Fuck off!" the driver growled.

The man stayed calm. His eyes didn't break contact. His hand rested on his blade.

"I'm sorry to bother you, but I was wondering if I could ask you a couple of questions?"

"I said—"

The man jabbed the driver in his throat with the punch dagger he had clipped to his belt. The driver's body tensed from the impact. Blood sprayed as the man's hand repositioned, releasing the pressure from the artery he'd just cut. He stabbed him again. And again. And again, his mind and body almost in a frenzy. It'd been a long time since he cut through the soft tissue of another being.

The feeling released something inside him. He felt a rush of adrenaline run through his body. He felt himself getting excited. He stopped. The driver slumped over towards the side. He wasn't dead, not yet. The man watched the driver take shallow breaths as blood poured out onto the passenger seat and in between. His head hung over to the side, his jacket opened, partially revealing the phone in his pocket. The man grabbed it. Inspected it. Placed it inside of a baggy. Then headed inside the house.

The man took off his sneakers and left them at the door. Walking barefoot on the carpet, his footsteps made no noise.

His breathing slowed. His heartbeat calmed. He was a living ghost roaming through the darkness.

The man heard items being knocked over on the upper floor. He followed the sound up the stairs and into Amy's room, where he had dreamed of joining her just a night ago. He walked up behind the intruder and stood there for moment, breathing in his scent. The intruder smelled of cigarettes and alcohol. Very offensive smells.

The intruder stood up.

He caught the man's reflection in the mirror.

His eyes widened.

He started to turn around.

His hand went reaching for his waistband to get his gun, but he was too slow. The man grabbed his arm and broke it at the wrist. He kicked out one of the intruder's legs, breaking his balance. He grabbed the intruder by his hair as he went down and kneed him in the face. Blood shot from his nose as it broke. The intruder was out before he hit the ground. The man stood over his body. He bent down and whispered, "Hello."

...

People make a lot of unnecessary noise. I've come to realize that some people just like to hear themselves talk. Some do it just to show off, others do it to simply sound smarter than they are. But most people do it because they are annoying.

I remember I went to a movie theatre to see a film I was interested in. I had found that I actually liked to watch movies. Unfortunately, on this day, there were a group of very rude individuals in the audience ruining my experience. They seemed to think that the patrons of the theatre paid to hear them make noise.

They talked throughout the whole film, and I decided since my night was ruined that theirs should be, too. I followed them to their car. Knocked them out. Took their vehicle. Drove them to a very private location that had a very nice view of the entire city. Then waited for them to wake up.

When they did, I told them they could be as loud as they wanted now, and promised that by the morning, they would be the center of attention. I then set the car on fire and watched nearby, eating some sunflower seeds as they screamed and cooked inside of their car. I remember the moon. It was so beautiful that night. I don't think it'd ever been that blue.

Filling in the Blanks

The intruder woke up to a blurry environment. His head pounded. There was enormous pressure around his sinuses. His nose and the area around his eyes felt swollen. He could taste the blood dripping down from his lip. He was dizzy and disoriented and he labored to breathe.

He tried to move his head but the motion was painful. A shock ran down his neck. He sucked in air and blew as hard as he could and winced as he tried to clear his nose.

"I wouldn't do that," the man said from the corner of the room. He was putting items back where they were, cleaning up the mess caused by the intruder. He laid down plastic along the floors. The intruder looked around as much as his strained neck would allow him. The room actually looked cleaner than it did when he first walked in.

The man stood up and dusted himself off. "Your nose is broken. I can set it if you like."

"You need to let me go!" the intruder demanded.

"You made a mess in here. I had to clean it up. This plastic? I placed it down so I wouldn't mess up Amy's rug. I know how stressful it can be to get blood out of carpet," the man said matter-of-factly. He stood in the corner of the room near the window, covered in darkness. The moonlight shined on his glasses.

"What do you want?" the intruder asked.

"I want to know what you are doing here, among other things. Those questions will come in time."

"Do you know who I work for?" he growled.

"No. Not yet. I'm sure you will tell me, though. Would you like some water before we start?"

The intruder didn't answer. He just sat there staring and breathing as best he could through his broken nose. His mind was trying to come up with ways to get out of this situation, but the only thing that swirled through his thoughts was the pain from his headache.

"Okay. I guess we should start then," the man said.

"Start what?" the intruder asked in a broken voice.

"I believe all relationships should start with trust and honesty. And that's how I want to start this one. Because without those things, you have nothing. Do you agree?"

"Do I have a choice?" he asked.

"There is always a choice. You can choose to answer my questions or you can choose not to. If you choose not to, then your decision comes at a price. If you lie to me, your decision comes at a price. Do you understand?"

"Yeah," the intruder said slowly.

"Good. I also believe that time is a precious thing. It is important to know this because it is the one thing in this world that we cannot get back. Do you agree with that?"

"Yes."

"Very good. We are starting off nicely. So. This will be very simple. I will ask you a question. You will give me an answer. If you decide to be honest with me, you will not suffer."

Over the years. The man had learned that the threat of violence was sometimes even more effective than the act itself. The man also learned that people start to freak out when they have lost their freedom.

Strapping a person to a chair and showing them all the fun objects that will be used to hurt them always makes the weak-minded easier to squeeze information out of. The man watched the intruder's body language. He saw the slight tremble. The worried look. The averted eye contact. The intruder was thinking. Maybe even contemplating if he should plead for his life. He was nervous. And that told the man everything he needed to know about him. It meant he would make a deal simply just to save himself.

"I'm going to start by asking you a very simple question to test your understanding of what I just said. Okay?" The man paused and studied his prisoner's face. "What is your name?"

The intruder looked around the portion of the room he could see. He sighed and blew out more mucus from his nose.

"Billy," he spat.

The man sucked his teeth in disappointment. He moved past his prisoner and pushed a table over. He started placing items on it.

"Wait, wait, wait, wait." the intruder said, rocking in his seat.

The man placed the prisoner's gun on the table.

"WHOA! Wait! What are you doing? I told you my name! I told you. I TOLD YOU!" the intruder pleaded.

The man picked up a hammer and gripped it tightly. He examined it. Felt its weight as he turned and twirled it. He looked mesmerized.

"No, you didn't." the man said calmly, not taking his eyes off the hammer. He placed it down and grabbed another object that he concealed in his hand. "I asked for your name. The one that's on your birth certificate. The one your mother gave you. The one that is here, on your license," the man said, holding it up and pointing to it. "William Kemp Dewar." The man threw the license down on his prisoner's lap.

"'Billy' is what everybody calls me. Friends. Family. You said you wanted trust, right? Well, people I trust call me 'Billy'," William explained.

"But I didn't ask what other people called you. I asked you to tell me your name. I need you to understand this moving forward, William, that when I ask you a question, I require a direct and completely honest answer. You have to listen to what is being asked, instead of just listening to answer."

William gritted his teeth. He looked down towards his license. He had a sick look on his face.

The man leaned forward in the darkness, revealing part of his features. And in a whisper, he said, "You shouldn't leave your license on you. It gives people like me power over you."

The man leaned back. There was a moment of calm. And then in one swift move, the man swung the flat side of the hammer across William's face. Blood shot from his lip as his teeth bit down into the soft tissue. There was a sharp pain in his jaw, one that intensified as he clenched his teeth. "I hate to punish you over simple things William, but I really do need you to understand my reasoning. Nod if you do."

William wasn't sure about anything anymore. He wasn't sure how he ended up in this sitatuon, and grew more upset at himself the longer he thought about it. But one thing was for certain, he was starting to understand just how truly screwed he really was. He nodded slowly. His lip quivered under the stress of the growing situation.

"Good. Now. Who lives at 122 Wester Ross?"

William didn't answer.

"Your wife?"

"..."

"An ex?"

"..."

"Your mom?" There was a slight twitch on William's face. His expression betrayed him. "Your mom." The man confirmed. He took the license from William's lap and placed it on the table next to a knife.

"I'm going to make this simple, William. Here is what's going to happen. And because you strike me as a man who needs incentive, I'm going to give you some choices. I'm going to ask some questions, same as before. And all I will require is an honest answer. If you decide not to give me those answers, I will go to your mother's house and videotape me killing her. I won't stop there. I will find out information on each and every person that you ever cared about. All those close to you. And I will do the same to them. And once I am done doing that, then, and only then, will I kill you. And I will take my time doing it. And while I'm doing it, I will have the videos of what I did to your family playing. Do you understand?"

William nodded slowly. He had a look of disgust on his face. The man picked up a canteen container.

"Do you know what this is, William?"

"It's a jug. Stainless steel."

"Do you know what's inside of it?"

"No."

"It's lye. Do you know what lye does to the body, William?"

"Yes."

"Good. Because the longer you make me wait for my answers, the more I will be inclined to make you drink this. Do you want that to happen, William?"

"No."

"Good." The man placed his watch down and started a timer. "First question. Why are you here?"

"I was hired to find something."

"To find what?"

"A laptop."

"Why?"

"It has some information on it. Information a lot of people don't want getting out."

"People like your boss?"

"Yes."

The man walked out of William's field of vision. William heard things being moved around and shifted. When the man came back into view, he brandished the laptop. William's eyes lit up.

"You'd be amazed at what you can find when you clean up a little, as opposed to throwing things around." He paused for a moment to study William's face. His reaction. He wished he brought a camera to savor the moment. "What's on here and how does it connect to Amy?"

"—"

"Time's a-ticking, William."

William looked at the container then back towards the figure of the man. "The laptop has a list of names and accounts that the girl somehow got a hold of. She thought she could use it as leverage to get out of the life. My boss, Artur Vasiliev—"

"Who is Artur Vasiliev?" the man asked with curiosity.

William looked stumped by the question. "You're not familiar with him?"

"No. That's why I'm asking. What is his business?"

"He runs the adoption program."

"The what?"

"The adoption program," William said slower, pronouncing every syllable. "It's an underground program that allows people with money to buy other people for a night. Or if they have a lot of money—I mean *a lot*—they can keep them longer."

"For what purpose?"

"Desire. Whatever their sick little minds can come up with to fulfill their needs. Sex…torture. You name it."

The answer seemed to arouse something in the man. A strong emotion of anger. Jealousy. The thought of someone else touching Amy was wrong.

"So, is that what he did with Amy? He put her up for adoption?"

"He arranged for Amy to come and speak with him first and—" William turned his head. His eyes rested on the table with the jug. He swallowed hard.

"And what?" the man asked. His face was partially obscured by the shadows, but even still, William could see the glint in the man's eyes.

"He gave her a way out."

"Your boss killed her?"

"No. He allowed a bunch of people to adopt her. At no cost. They just had to let him watch and—"

The man cracked his neck. The noise unsettled William. The man then turned and faced one of the pictures that was on Amy's dresser, one that depicted Amy with a huge smile on her face. Laughing and having fun. Something she wouldn't be able to do again. Something she probably was never truly able to do. She would never be able to go on park dates with the man, or out to the mall, or put on shower shows for him while she touched herself. The man would never be able to smell her hair from up close.

"Listen, man. I'm just a grunt here. I do tech work. That's it. I get paid to do what I'm told. I have no ties to that girl. Me being here is just business. You understand, right?"

The man didn't respond to his prisoner. He was still looking at the photos. Still thinking about his loss.

"I get it. You two were close. She probably sucked you off or whatever. I don't know. But you're upset. I understand. But how about you and I strike a deal, huh? That laptop has all kinds of bank accounts on it. Underground money. You found it, you take it. And I can just leave and say I never found it. And that I never saw you. How does that sound?"

The man thought of what William had said. *Desire.* The man thought of his dream and how he was drowning Amy in it. The man wondered if Artur would like that, or better yet, if Artur had a loved one that he would like to watch die. The man had fallen deep into his thoughts.

The timer went off, breaking the man from his trance. He stretched his neck to the side, cracking it again. He adjusted his glasses and examined his reflection in the mirror. His face was void of emotion, even though inside, his anger was growing.

He felt it swarming up like a mass of bees, turning him into something monstrous. He felt his hands grip tightly into a fist. He had failed Amy. He was supposed to keep her safe until he could get to her.

He remembered the promise he made to her in one of his daydreams. He'd imagined their wedding day. He told her he would never let anything or anyone hurt her. She smiled at his words and reached her hand out. And when he shook it, he knew right then and there she would be his forever. A promise that had now turned into a lie. A skeleton of death.

They had taken her away. They had made a mistake.

"Listen, man. Listen! I told you what you wanted to know, all right? Just let me go, please. I have kids. And my mom is sick and I'm the only one who can take care of her. Please."

William's words were distant. Far away from thought. All the man could hear were his own deliberations that thrashed around in his head. He felt the darkness of the room cover his body and clamp onto his mind.

The man's eyes glanced over at the bottle of lye.

He turned slowly towards William and stared down at him with contempt. And in one swift motion, the man hit William in his throat with his hand.

William gasped for air. The man then grabbed William's broken nose and twisted it as he reached for the canteen and poured its contents into William's mouth. William's eyes shot open. Tears rolled down his face as he involuntarily swallowed the burning chemicals that ate at his flesh. William choked and thrashed as the liquids splashed around on his face and neck and down into his stomach. His body jerked and twitched and spasmed as the man held him down.

The last thing William recalled before losing consciousness was seeing the man's vacant face. Cold. Cold as the night air.

...

People sometimes forget that there's no meaning to life. That it's just some cruel joke that God came up with. In the end, we all die. Some of us go naturally. Others? Not so naturally. Whatever the case, we all try to find ways to outlive our end dates.

People plead and fight. They hide. They beg.

They even make deals with other people's lives in exchange for their own. These are the worst kinds of people. The ones who care solely about themselves. I've found there is no end to their treachery.

I once had a man offer the lives of his family in exchange for his own life. It begged me to ask the question: how many lives are worth the life of one? The answer? Zero.

Why trade for something that you can get for free?

Why buy something that has already exceeded its expiration?

Daniel Moretti

Daniel Moretti wasn't the most respected man in the criminal world. He started running the business after his father died. However, his father, who was known for his cruelty and power, lacked something Daniel had become a master at: having resources and connections in the right places. These things, and these things alone, made working with Daniel Moretti bearable.

He was headed to meet Detective Swanson at the city morgue. The detective said he needed to show him something. Whatever it was, Moretti knew he didn't want to see it. The morgue wasn't the kind of place he liked to go visit for the hell of it. He walked into the room. It was cold. Sterile. He squinted as his eyes adjusted to the fluorescent lights. The detective stood in the middle of the room and leaned against the metal slab with his arms folded. His face was impassive. Behind him was a body that laid under a sheet and on top of a metal table.

"Good morning, detective. How are things?"

"Could be better!"

"Yeah, I'm sure. You pulled me out of an important meeting to stand here among the dead. I'm guessing this is important?"

The detective turned and removed the sheet from over the body. "Is this Joshua?" the detective asked. There was a hint of annoyance in his voice.

Moretti glanced over at the body, then back at the detective. "Yeah. Congratulations. You found him. You brought me all the way down here to ID a body?" Moretti said sharply.

Swanson glared at him. "No. We have a problem. And I need your help with gaining some insight on how to fix it."

"You want me to help you fix a problem?" Moretti scoffed. "Fixing problems is your department. That's why the fine citizens of this city pay taxes. Not so they can do your job for you. It's so you can go out there and fix the problems of the city yourself. Me? I handle businesses—a club. This," Moretti said, pointing at the body, "has nothing to do with me."

"It does when the dead guy worked at your club. A club which engages in criminal activity, human trafficking, and prostitution, to name a few. It involves you when your club, as of recently, is the center of a fucking scandal."

Moretti rubbed his chin and gave Swanson a sly grin. "Again. Nothing to do with me. That was your boss's decision to have the girl killed before getting what he needed."

"Yes, it was. But it was you who offered her up. Because, let's not forget, it was you who was telling this slut all our secrets. Feeding her information and giving her access to things because she was fucking you!" Swanson snapped.

Moretti shrugged his shoulders. "Hey. Who knew she was smart enough to start blackmailing us?"

"Yeah, 'who knew.'"

"Speaking of which," Moretti said, moving closer to Swanson, who scrunched up his face in disgust. "Did your guys find it?"

"No. Because, 'speaking of which,' the guys who went to find it are dead." Swanson watched as the understanding crept into Moretti's little rat eyes.

"Really?"

"Yes, really!" Swanson said, squaring up to Moretti.

Moretti's hands went up in an act of compliance. "Whoa. Hey. I had nothing to do with that, if that's what you're thinking."

"No, I know you didn't have anything to do with it," Swanson hissed. "If I thought you did, we wouldn't be having this conversation."

"Right."

"You wanna know how they died?"

Moretti shook his head.

"Of course, you do."

"No, I'm pretty sure I don't." And that was the truth. The whole situation was turning into a nightmare. Moretti's whole world was turning upside down. He was free-diving face first into the concrete.

"Some asshole walked into a public place and locked your boy here in a sauna and turned the heat all the way up. Whoever it was…the cocksucker was nice enough to leave him a cup of water next to the door."

"Yeah. I kind of said I didn't want to know."

"Jimmy was stabbed so many times in the throat, his head was practically hanging off."

"…and you're still telling me."

"And Billy was tied to a fucking chair and had lye poured down his mouth. The poor bastard coughed up bits of his insides. The parts that didn't end up in his lap dissolved in his stomach!"

"With all due respect, detective, I'm not sure what you aim to accomplish by telling me these things."

Swanson puffed out his chest and glared down into Moretti's face. "Listen, you little weasel. I need to know who else you might have been talking to. Who else might have been sucking information out of you. Who else might have known about this laptop. Who you might have pissed off lately."

Moretti scoffed. "Who *I* might have pissed off? Take your pick. I have enemies everywhere. Everyone wants a piece of what I have. Maybe even your boys in blue. Mad because I have people like you working for me."

"I don't work for you, Moretti. I work for Artur Vasiliev. And right now, Mr. Vasiliev isn't too happy about this sudden turn of events. You should feel lucky you're talking to me and not him," Swanson countered.

Moretti smiled. "Don't stand here and try to make *me* out to be some kind of rat-snitch, alright? Acting all high and mighty. I didn't tell anybody anything. Amy was a screw-up, I know, and that was my bad, but—"

"What about Amy? Did she have anyone else she was seeing? Anyone she might have been working with? Talking to?"

"No. I mean, she had clients. Most of my top girls do. I doubt she had anybody else involved with her, though. I don't—" Moretti paused. His face had a look of something in between shock and concentration, as if something had just smacked him in the face.

"What? You don't what?" Swanson asked, confused.

"That…a guy. There was a guy. The other night."

"What guy?" Swanson queried.

"At the club! Joshua said that some guy came and…Shit!"

"What? If you got something, spit it out, Moretti!"

"Some guy came into the club the other night. The night that, you know…when your people took care of Amy. Joshua said he came in and started asking about her. Said he was looking around all worried and left abruptly when he was told Amy wasn't there."

"And you didn't think that was important?"

"Not really. I had my guys look into it."

"And?"

"And nothing. They said the guy was a nobody. One of my men recognized him. Said he worked at the local shopping center."

"A fucking nobody?"

"Yeah. What? At the time, it didn't seem important."

"I decide what's important and what's not," Swanson said, pointing his finger into Moretti's chest. "Me. Not you. Me. Some guy starts asking about a dead person that no one should even notice is gone, and now I have dead bodies popping up all over the place. It's the 'nobodies' I worry about. They're the ones you don't see coming!" He turned his head and looked off into the distance at nothing. "What did this nobody look like?"

"Joshua said he was maybe six feet. Slim build. Said he was dressed in slacks and a button-up shirt. Bald head. Wore glasses."

"Black, white, Hispanic?"

"Black," Moretti answered quickly.

Swanson shook his head. "A fucking nobody," he repeated.

"I get your point."

"You don't, Moretti. See, Artur is worried about this situation because it's a big pile of shit that he's stepped in, thanks to you. Now we all have to suffer. But trust this: if this situation doesn't get handled in a way that meets Mr. Vasiliev's satisfaction, it'll be your ass on the line."

"Don't threaten me," Moretti said in a voice that betrayed him.

Swanson smiled, then leaned closer and said, "That's not a threat." He looked him up and down, and saw Moretti sweating. "Your club still have that surveillance system?"

"Yeah, why?"

"Because I'm going to want the footage. All of it. I'll see if I can get something off the city cameras as well. I got a guy that works in the traffic division that can do it discreetly. Also, I'm going to call my guys. They'll probably be by to question—"

"Your guys?" Moretti scoffed.

"Yes, my guys."

"Those Spanish fucks? Last time you used them, they left a bigger mess than what we started with."

"First of all, they're Colombian; Spanish is a language. Secondly, they always get the job done. Not only that, but they don't exist inside of our world, inside of our rules. That's a very valuable asset to have when you need things done discreetly. Someone who is invisible and efficient."

Moretti scoffed. He didn't care how good they were. All he could think about was all the money he might lose having them involved.

"You do understand the need to keep this whole thing

quiet, right?" Swanson asked. "We don't want anything leading back to anyone, because if it does, no one walks away."

"You don't want anything leading back to your boys in blue. You don't want the public to find out just how culpable their beloved police force is. Can you imagine how this city would fall if they knew the mob ran the local law enforcement?"

"I think you're letting your ego get in the way of the bigger picture, Moretti. Joshua was killed in a public place. He was found by the gym's employees. That was a bitch to clean up. The other two? Easy. You know why? No civilian eyes involved. We need to keep everything we do tight and off the books. And we also need to be careful. Because if my gut is correct, then we're dealing with a professional. My past experience tells me that it's best to let killers handle other killers. So. I'm going to call my guys. They're going to do their investigation, which will include talking to you and your employees. And hopefully we can have all this wrapped up sooner rather than later."

"And the laptop?" Moretti asked.

Swanson's face twitched in annoyance at the question—because the very person who put him in this situation stood right in front of him. But even still, Swanson couldn't ignore the importance of having this item in his hands.

"We'll find it. For your sake. And mine."

The Escobar Brothers

L ucas's and Diego's last names weren't Escobar. They weren't even real brothers. They just liked the term, which was given to them after they did some hits for a cartel. Now they did work for whomever contracted them, turning Escobar Brothers into a name, a business, one that dealt with death.

Lucas was playing guitar as someone screamed in the background. He had a scar on his throat from an old war wound that robbed him of his speech. When the phone rang, he looked over towards his brother and signed for him to get it. Diego walked over in a butcher's outfit covered in blood. He picked up the phone.

"Hello?"

"I need something packaged and delivered to me. Will pay for shipping."

"Okay. When do you need it by?"

"The sooner the better."

"We'll be in contact." Diego hung up the phone.

Lucas scratched his face and signed, "Who was it?"

"Swanson. Needs us to do a job. He sounded a bit stressed," Diego said as he walked back to finish what he was doing. He stood in front of a man who hung upside down from the ceiling. Diego picked up a drill and grabbed the hanging man by his jaw. Blood seeped from his mouth. Diego turned on the drill and got to work on his teeth. He spoke over the man's screams. "I'll notify Rafael and Javier, and let them know where to meet us. We can head there once I'm done." Diego wasn't sure what the job Swanson wanted done entailed, but the stress in his voice told Diego that he should probably add a couple more bodies to their two-man team.

Swanson sent over the details of their assignment, which seemed easy enough. It was a simple snatch and grab. Swanson needed someone interrogated. Apparently, someone was killing his guys and was possibly also in possession of something he needed. Lucas thought a job like this was somewhat beneath them. But after he saw the photos of what the guy did, he was intrigued.

They had little information on their suspect. Black male. Possibly six feet. Slim, athletic build. Bald head. Wore glasses and drove a Volkswagen. Lucas had an odd feeling about this. It wasn't just that the guy's plates came back to someplace from upstate. But the security photos that Swanson had sent showed a guy who looked very out of place.

At first, second, and third glance, the man didn't seem like much. He definitely didn't seem like the kind of guy that would do the things Lucas saw in those photos. But in Lucas's line of work, he learned two things: never judge a book by its cover and never judge. Period. That's not what he was getting paid to do. His job was to capture the man so Diego could question him. Diego was good at questioning.

Their first stop into town was the strip club. They didn't go in. Lucas stood outside watching the place from a distance, becoming one with the energies around him. They then went to both crime scenes and did the same thing there, except this time, Lucas went inside. He walked into the gym and into the men's locker room and stood in front of the sauna. On Amy's street, he walked up the block and stood on the sidewalk in front of the house. He then went inside. He walked up the stairs and entered Amy's room. He stood next to the stains on the floor and closed his eyes. He then walked silently back to the car and they drove to their next stop, the shopping center. Their target supposedly worked at Smart Shop. They walked around the store to get a feel of the place. Minutes later, they found the manager's office door and knocked. It opened up to Michael sitting at his desk.

"Yes, may I—"

"Help us? Yes, please. My brother and I would appreciate that much," Diego said with a thick accent. Michael looked up at the large man who pretty much took up the whole space in his doorway.

Diego held up a picture. "Does this man work here?" he asked.

Michael squinted at the photo. "Yes, he does," Michael said sharply. He was thrown off by their abrasiveness.

Diego placed the photo back into his pocket. "Is he working here today?"

"No. He has been off sick," the manager said defensively.

"Oh, okay. Well, would you mind giving us some more information on him? Maybe tell us where we could get in contact with him?"

Michael leaned over to look around Diego. His eyes set on Lucas, who stood there, mute. He saw the scar that went around his neck. He had tattoos that seemed to cover most of his body. He even had some on his face. Michael sat back in his chair. "I'm sorry. Can I ask what this is pertaining to?"

"Yes, you may. We work at the gentlemen's club on Connecticut Street. Are you familiar with it?"

"I am."

"I'm sure you are. Anyway, this man left some things there that we would like to give back to him."

"You can leave it with me. I can give it to him when he comes back."

"We were kind of hoping to give it to him in person, see—"

"I'm sorry, I don't want to further waste your time, gentlemen. I can't give you any information on any employee. I've probably told you too much already. If David lost something somewhere, you are more than welcome to leave it here. Otherwise, just wait until he comes back to work or visits your place of business."

Diego's eyes said many things as he stood and stared at Michael. None of them were good things. His mouth decided on something else.

"Thank you. We will do that." He stepped out of the office. Michael closed the door and as he did, Lucas turned to glance at him one final time and saw that he was getting on the phone. They started to walk out of the store when—

"Did you say you were looking for David?" a woman's voice

asked from behind them. The brothers turned around to face a petite woman.

Her name tag read *Kristen*.

Package Delivery

The man sat in his house looking through Amy's laptop. He wasn't interested in the accounts. Or the blackmail, for that matter. What he wanted was basic information. Names. Places. He went through every list on the drive and memorized everything about everyone that was on it. He found that all of them were linked to one person: Artur Vasiliev.

He started to piece together a profile for Mr. Vasiliev. His family was tied to the mob. He owned various properties and businesses around Tupper Falls, New York. One of the major ones was a law firm. But the most interesting form of income came from his hotel, Artur Suites. The building was located in the heart of Tupper Falls in the downtown district. The hotel was a front, however. Underneath it was, aptly, an underground club, exclusive to the affluent. His adoption program, a place where people could live out their fantasies with unwilling participants. The man scoffed at the idea. Having someone do all the hunting for you while they served up your prize like a frozen dinner was such a lazy way to kill, the man thought.

He pulled up a picture of Artur and his family. He had a wife and son. A beautiful, happy family. He rubbed his hand along the laptop screen, then laid his face against it. He would be seeing Artur soon, and his family shortly after. Maybe even at the same time, if he was lucky.

The man stood up and went down to his basement and grabbed a dry-erase board and some Post-its. He grabbed a map of the city and placed it on the board. He started jotting down notes and times. Dates and people. Circling locations.

He printed out photos of all the players and did further research on them, gathering as much intel as his brain could take. He was starting to feel happy. Something was awakening inside him and it felt good. He felt at home. And for once, he felt almost normal. He couldn't wait to meet all his new friends. He couldn't wait to show them things. He especially couldn't wait to meet Mr. Vasiliev. He drew a circle around Mr. Vasiliev's face and then, his doorbell rang.

The man looked over at his monitor switching the screen to the security camera. There was a person holding an envelope at the door. He was dressed in street clothes. The man walked over.

"Yes?" the man asked through the crack of the door.

"I have a package for David Johnson. Is he here?" the person said.

The man took his time answering. He thought the question was odd, mainly because he knew David Johnson hadn't ordered anything. "Leave it on the porch."

"I would like to hand it to him, please." The person looked behind the man, into the house.

The man opened the door fully. He stood there for a moment examining him.

The delivery guy shifted slightly and averted the man's eyes. "I have a package for—"

"Yes. You said that," the man said, keeping his stare. He knew he was breaking his rules again but at this point, he had already broken more than one of them.

"Yes. I did," the delivery man replied. He handed the man an envelope.

The man looked at it impassively. "What's inside this?"

"A present to you, from a friend," he said, giving the man a devious grin. He back-stepped off the porch, keeping his stare and his smile locked onto the man.

The man closed his door. He opened up the envelope and took out a thumb drive. He examined it as he walked over to his computer and inserted it. He found a file titled "The Pieces of Amy."

The man grabbed a bag of sunflower seeds and started eating them as he opened the file. There were photos of what looked like a hotel room. There was blood on the walls. Blood on the floor mixed with chunks of flesh. On the bed was a body, mutilated to an unrecognizable degree. The man placed some seeds into his mouth and spat the shells into a separate baggie. He clicked through the photos slowly.

Most of them were close-up shots. Red marks along Amy's neck and chest. Bruising along her torso. Her private parts had been mutilated. Her nipples cut off. Dried blood ran down her bruised thighs. Her fingers had been cut off, along with her tongue and ears. Her eyes swollen shut. The man placed more seeds in his mouth and spat more shells into the bag. He sat back in his chair, closed the file, and stared blankly at the screen. He adjusted his glasses and opened his music app and played a nice piano piece with a relaxing violin and cello overlay. He then double-clicked the file again and started from the top.

Come In

Lucas watched as Javier came running back towards the van after delivering the package. But his mind wasn't focused on him. Instead, he was looking at the house, towards the area where Rafael was stationed. There was something about this whole thing that bothered him. The energy felt… off. David. And everything about him. Was off. Even now.

Lucas stared at David's house. Its clean shade of blue with its white trim. The short-cut grass. The Volkswagen that sat in the driveway, shiny as if brand new. The lawn ornaments that decorated the front. Almost everything seemed…too perfect. Like something you'd see in a movie. It made Lucas uneasy. Which, for him, was rare.

As Javier entered the van, Diego turned in his driver seat, facing him.

"Well?" Diego asked.

"Yeah, it's him. We going in?"

Diego looked back at Lucas for confirmation. Lucas signed his answer, his eyes locked on the house. Diego scoffed and sat forward in his seat, waving him off dismissively.

"What did he say?" Javier asked.

"He said we need to wait," Diego responded.

"Wait for what?"

"For Rafael." There was a ding and a vibration that came from Diego's pocket. He took out his phone then smiled. A text came through Diego's phone from Rafael. He glanced at the message and looked back at Lucas.

"Rafael said he's at the back of the house. Says he's ready to move when you are." Lucas shook his head. Something wasn't right. He signed to Diego, who scoffed a laugh in reply. Javier looked confused.

"What's going on?"

"He's spooked," Diego teased. "Thinks something is off with the spirits and energies. Thinks we should wait."

"Wait for what?"

"Who knows. Maybe for the stars to align correctly," Diego mocked.

Lucas shook his head.

"What do you think?" Javier asked.

"I think it's one guy against four of us. And the four of us are like twenty. I think we should just grab him and get it over with so we can collect our pay."

Lucas glared at his friend. Diego never had a real sense for danger. He liked to rush into things. His size often allowed for that. Lucas, on the other hand, liked to follow his instincts. And right now, his gut was telling him to gather more information before acting.

Lucas looked over towards the house and saw that the front door was open. He banged his hand against the car, alerting the others. Diego turned his head. He looked over towards the house. Seeing the open door, he glanced at Lucas and smiled.

"I guess we're going in."

Kill Squad

Diego stepped out of the van and made his way towards the house. He scrutinized the windows and the door, clearing the space before he walked closer. Javier followed behind him, his gun raised. Lucas made his way towards the back of the house. Diego and Javier entered from the front. And as Diego stepped into the living room, he paused.

Rafael was sitting slumped over on the couch. His hands were resting palm-up on his lap. Each hand held one of his eyeballs. Rafael's lower jaw was nearly hanging off from a cut that went from ear to ear, giving him a crimson smiley face.

Diego walked over, drew an invisible cross on his chest, then placed his hand on his comrade's shoulder. He bowed his head and said a small prayer. Javier stood frozen, his gaze held on Rafael.

He heard a voice, whisper.

"You should check your corners."

Javier's eyes went wide as he shifted nervously, fumbling with his gun as he tried to spin around. And as he did, his body jolted, then stopped as the man stabbed him.

He felt the cold metal slip inside his body, hitting him twice in the liver. The knife slid across his abdomen, opening his belly. He felt the warmth of his insides slide out of him with a hiss of air and moisture. Javier's gun hit the floor. His body followed, giving a loud thump.

Diego registered the noise.

He turned around and started shooting. The man grabbed Javier, lifting him up. He used him as a shield, side-stepping as he held the limp body in front of him.

The bullets whipped through the air.

The man kept coming forward, feeling the impact of the rounds that tore into his cover of flesh.

He heard the sound of Diego's gun clicking and locking back.

The man dropped the body. He lunged at Diego, who just smiled as their bodies collided. Diego stared into the man's empty, expressionless face. He felt a rage build up in his chest. He grabbed the man by his throat and exploded into a roar of anger as he slammed the man into the wall.

The man grabbed at Diego's large arms. He tried pulling at his grip. He tried pushing him off, but Diego only held him tighter. The man was a wolf, trapped in the arms of a bear. Diego smiled maniacally as he used his size to bully the smaller man. He lifted him up and slammed him into a nearby desk, pinning the man down as he jammed his elbow into his face.

"I'm going to enjoy cutting pieces off of you," Diego

taunted. "I will save your eyes for last, so you can see everything I do. Or maybe I take them first, and let you guess what pain is to come next. One thing is for sure; when I'm done, you will roam around hell. Blind and broken."

The man didn't stir. His face was apathetic to the whole ordeal, almost bored. He reached onto his belt and gripped his punch dagger between his fingers. He made his hand into a fist, then jammed the blade into the underside of Diego's arm, tearing into Diego's armpit as he twisted and pulled the blade out and in, repeating the motion over and over again until Diego released him.

Diego pushed the man back.

He touched himself and felt his wounds.

His hands came back with blood.

He felt it run down his side. Warm and slick. He couldn't see what damage was done, but he knew an artery was cut from the amount of blood that was rushing down his side.

He was already starting to feel woozy.

His arm hung down limply.

He looked over at the man and lunged at him, swinging with his good arm. But the motion was useless.

The man kicked out Diego's kneecap. It made a loud popping sound as Diego's weight gave out, twisting his leg at a weird angle. The man stomped on Diego's ankle, breaking it.

Diego screamed out in pain as his body collapsed to the floor. The man grabbed Diego's hair and pulled his head back.

"Diablo," Diego said as he looked up at the man, who gave him a vile smirk in response, as if he was enjoying this. The man examined Diego's neck for a moment, then started punching Diego in his throat repeatedly with the dagger.

Blood splattered onto the man's face.

It stained his clothes.

Diego gurgled and choked on his blood.

A gunshot exploded from the doorway, grazing the man's shoulder. The man turned his head and looked over at Lucas who was aiming his gun, preparing to shoot again.

Last Man Standing

The man swiftly dived to the side just as the bullets came flying towards him. He rolled aside and disappeared deeper into the house.

Lucas's face was a mask of pain and anger. He crouched down towards his friend. His partner, his brother. Diego's breathing was shallow. Lucas placed his hand on Diego's chest and felt his friend's life slip away. He wiped off Diego's blood, then stood up and slowly crept through the living room. The floorboards creaked underneath his feet.

Lucas stayed close to the wall, creeping slowly, then stopped at the edge. He took a deep breath in, mentally preparing himself. He quickly maneuvered around it, aiming his gun. There was nothing there but consuming dread and a sinking feeling in his gut, that he was in danger.

Lucas didn't hear the man coming up behind him.

But he felt him.

His presence was undeniable.

It was that same horrible presence he felt creeping into his soul prior to their coming into the house. It was as if the man's aura was its own separate entity, corrupting the world around it.

Lucas gritted his teeth and spun around as quickly as he could. He swung his gun around at the same time and aimed at the man, who grabbed his arm and stopped his momentum. The man then slammed a hammer down onto Lucas's hands, freeing the gun from him. He went to strike again, but Lucas moved. Knocking the hammer from the man's grip. He then pushed into the man, forcing him back as Lucas threw a series of punches.

The man bobbed and weaved, dodging the blows.

He ducked under a looping hook, reached inside of his shirt and produced a knife, then rammed it into Lucas's inner thigh, who buckled from the impact. The man kicked out Lucas's leg, dropping him to the floor, then casually walked over to the hammer, picked it up, and swung it furiously into Lucas's kneecap. There was an audible cracking sound as the metal hit the bone.

Lucas let out a scream, but it came out hushed and strained against his damaged vocal cords. His face twisted in pain. Lucas grabbed his leg as he rested against the wall, bracing himself with his good arm just as the man came down with the hammer again, slamming it onto Lucas's collarbone.

The man stood there for a moment, watching Lucas as he tried and failed to stay standing. The sight of it made the man crack a smile, and for once, it felt genuine. Lucas continued to struggle to stay upright. He looked at the man, glaring into his eyes with a hatred he didn't know he possessed. He slid all the way down onto the floor, letting his body go, accepting his fate.

The man knelt down next to him. Lucas knew this was it. He knew he was at the mercy of a sadist. He spat blood in the man's face, defiant to the end. The man didn't flinch. In fact, it was if he hadn't even noticed. He simply reached out and rubbed his fingers along the scar that circled Lucas's neck.

"I know you can't talk," the man said softly. "But I'm curious to know if you can scream."

There was something about the man's eyes. Something that sparked in them. Something that was wrong inside of them. Lucas had felt fear before, but this…this was different. There was something endless in the man. Something that took joy in the chaos. A violence that had no stop to its hunger. A monster that did not belong here among the living. He was not a man. He was a force that Lucas realized, far too late, should not have been roused.

"I'm going to stay away from your fingers," the man said, looking Lucas over, "because I know you need those to communicate. I'm hoping you will be kind enough to answer the questions I have for you." The man stood up and walked over towards the fridge and poured himself a glass of water. He looked over towards Lucas before taking a sip and asked, "Would you like something to drink?"

...

I've always loathed rude people, but I have also always found some use for them. I remember once a man cut me off on the road. This was around the time I decided to stop killing people. I didn't follow him at first. We just happened to be going in the same direction.

I remember thinking maybe this was a sign. Maybe fate wanted me to follow this man. Incidentally, we ended up at his home. Or a place that I initially thought was his home. After spending about a week following him around and getting to know him, I learned that this place was actually his mistress's house. I found this also to be rude.

To do something behind his loved one's back was a terrible thing. I decided to meet this person up close and have a talk with him about honor, respect, and loyalty. And most importantly, etiquette. I also had his lady friend there to be educated as well.

That night, I believe my friend learned a lot of things. But the most important lesson he learned, I guess, was for him to use his turn signals, and not cut people off when they have the right of way.

It's not nice.

Purpose

The **man** stood facing the mirror in the basement of his home. He thought about the events that brought him to this moment. He wiped his face, smearing it with blood. He needed to see himself clearly. The man spent his entire life wearing masks, and never once had he stopped and thought about who the person was underneath them, what he truly wanted, or what his purpose was.

Before the man's mother died, she wanted him to find his purpose. To do and be something she could be proud of. That was part of the reason he'd sacrificed his urges, for the sake of becoming a man. The man thought he'd achieved that. Yet, despite all his progress, fate had decided to bring him back to this person he stands before now. The one whose reflection is broken. A man beyond whom he'd set out to be. And it felt right.

It was tiring for the man to try to be someone else, someone he wasn't, someone stuck inside of a hollow husk. Dying one day at a time, realizing that every second he spent being nothing was just another moment he'd be closer to accepting the mediocrity of his existence, realizing that life was nothing more than a series of repeated tasks. Balance was a tricky thing to master.

A text message popped up on Diego's phone. The man looked at it with curious eyes.

"Was my package delivered?" the message read. The man knew it was Detective Swanson, mainly because Lucas told him so. Lucas had told the man a lot of things. The man stretched his neck towards the side and cracked it.

"Yes," the man replied with bloody fingers.

"Good. Any issues?"

"Yes. A few," the man replied again.

The man placed the phone down and looked at his reflection again. His features were blank, his body simply a shadow waiting to return to the night. He knew what he needed to do.

The man walked over towards his storage and took out a box labeled "David Johnson." He placed the box on the floor in his room. He then carried Rafael's body and laid it down neatly on his bed, tucking him in under the covers. He grabbed a pair of pliers and got to work on Rafael's mouth, taking the teeth out of the upper jaw and removing the lower one completely. When he was finished, he started removing the contents from his box. Inside he had hair fibers, a jawline with teeth, and articles of clothing. He took the teeth out and placed them near the body.

The man went back to his basement, where he had several containers full of gasoline. He was glad he saved them and experienced a warm feeling travel through his body—he thought he would never have any use for them again. He brought them upstairs, and emptied the contents over his furniture, the floors, and throughout the house. The man took a match from his pocket and lit his house on fire. He stood there for a moment inside of his doorway and watched the blaze eat away at the life he had worked hard to attain. He said a soft goodbye then left. The man then took the clothing and hair fibers with him and placed them throughout his Volkswagen.

The man got into the Escobar brothers' van. He placed a locked box on the passenger's seat. Inside was something he held dear, something he'd hidden away years before, something that was as much a part of him as his own skin.

He opened the box. There was a handcrafted white mask with poor humanoid features that formed a devilish grin. The man rubbed his fingers along the rugged edges, admiring the off-putting features. A soft banging erupted from the trunk.

The man closed the lockbox. His face would have to wait. He still had more things to ask Lucas. And after their play time was over, he would head over to Artur's playhouse, where the real fun would begin.

The Fire

It was late in the day when Swanson got the call about a fire. He rushed over to the scene. He wasn't sure why or how it happened, but he hadn't planned on a fire breaking out. The Escobars were supposed to take the man to an undisclosed location. Someplace private, a place Swanson wouldn't have to worry about cleaning up. But now Swanson had a bad feeling, one that got worse as he neared his destination. The Escobar brothers had contacted him, but he couldn't help but feel a sense of dread. A fire, he feared, meant something went horribly wrong.

Or maybe not.

Maybe this was a blessing and a curse. Because a fire also meant there would be no need to clean up the scene. Most or probably all of the evidence would be destroyed, leaving his peers to speculate. But that was the issue: his peers.

Other people were now involved.

Fire. Neighbors. Witnesses. And then there was the other issue he was avoiding.

Artur Vasiliev's people had tried several times to get in contact with Swanson, and each time Swanson ignored them. Swanson knew that wasn't going to go over well. They wanted an update on the situation. But the truth was, Swanson didn't have one.

He still didn't have the laptop, he still didn't have the whole Amy situation cleaned up. And now, things were more than likely going to be all over the news. Everything was spiraling out of control and Swanson was neck-deep in it with no way out. All because he wanted to make a little extra money on the side to beef up his pension. He shouldn't have gotten involved, not with criminals. He shouldn't have gotten greedy.

Swanson had placed himself in a situation that could very well blow up in his face. If the information on that laptop got out, he would have to live the rest of his life looking over his shoulder. The skeletons in his closet still had meat on them. The secrets were adding up. Overflowing. All Internal Affairs needed was a whiff of something rotten, and they would be all over it. His career would be over and jail would not be a good environment for him. But in comparison, jail was a much better place than anywhere Artur Vasiliev would put him. That laptop needed to be found. And it needed to be found now. His only hope was that by some chance, this David person had it and it was destroyed in this fire. But that was assuming fate was on his side. So far, his track record showed that it wasn't.

He pulled up to the scene.

Multiple fire trucks blocked off the street along with some

police vehicles. There were two fire investigators and another homicide detective standing next to a couple of civilians. The detectives were taking notes, which meant they had witnesses. Swanson cringed. He knew the chances of this getting back to him were slim, but he couldn't help but feel a bit nervous about the whole ordeal. He liked to keep things quiet, and this was not quiet. He gathered his thoughts and did his best to ease his nerves as he walked over and met his colleagues. His eyes scanned around for Internal Affairs. He wasn't expecting them to be there, but his paranoia was taking over.

"About time you got here, Swanson," a female detective said. "You know how long we've been trying to reach you?"

"Yeah, I've been busy. What do we have?" He glanced over towards the house. Firefighters had put out the fire, but were still tearing at the foundation of the house, hosing down smoking wood.

"House fire," she said as she took a sip of her coffee.

"Yeah, I see that. Anything else? Why was I called here?"

"Three bodies."

"Three?" Swanson said. His voice sounded more surprised than intended.

"Yeah. Three. You sound shocked," she accused, giving him a curious look.

"No. I mean…" he shrugged his shoulders. "I just wasn't expecting that. Any evidence for us or did the fire destroy it?"

"Well, we got something," she said smiling. "We're going to take the car."

"Why?"

"The VIN number doesn't match the plates."

"It doesn't?"

"No, it doesn't."

"What does it match up to?"

"The plates come back to a David Johnson out of Middletown, New York."

"And the VIN?"

"Comes back to a lady from, get this, Toronto."

"Canada?"

"Yeah," she said with a hard grin.

"That's weird."

"It gets weirder. We got a hit on David's name. He was reported missing five years ago."

"Really?"

"Yeah."

The detective's name was Angela. Swanson didn't care much for her. She did everything by the book, which always made her a little overeager to get things done a certain way. But still, he had to admit, the information she was giving him was helpful. Information that, if Swanson had done things by the book, he would've had by now.

Swanson scratched his head. "So…what? This guy goes AWOL, travels to Ontario, steals a car and then comes to live here? Why?" Swanson was very curious about this Canada detail.

"Think he was hiding from someone?" Angela asked.

"Hiding?"

"Yeah. Take a look at this." She moved closer to Swanson until they were shoulder to chest. She hit the screen on her tablet and pulled up the images she took from inside the house. Swanson stood there staring at a picture of a crispy husk. Two of them. She slid her finger across the screen to show a different angle of the room. This one had a better view. On the floor between the bodies were shell casings.

"Here's what I came up with so far. This guy Johnson gets into some kind of trouble with some bad people. So bad that he has to move away. He gets a place here. Starts over. These guys track him down. A struggle ensues here in the living room. I'm guessing he gets the drop on these two and a third guy takes him out in his bedroom."

"What makes you think it's three guys?" Swanson asked, trying to mask his worry with interest.

Angela had a smirk on her face, one Swanson had come to loathe. Angela swiped over towards a picture of the bedroom. There was a body on the bed, burned beyond recognition.

"We found teeth in the master bedroom. The top ones had been pulled out one by one. The lower jaw was removed completely then discarded to the side. An attack like that… it's personal. Whoever did it wanted to make an example out of him. We collected the teeth and sent them to the lab. The results haven't come back in yet, but I bet you my pension they end up matching with this David guy. And if that's so, that can only mean there was one other person there to have did it. So, unless the victim developed some complicated way to murder himself by torture and fire, I'm going to confidently say there's another guy out there."

"That's a solid theory," Swanson agreed.

And it was. It had some holes in it, but given the circumstances, this was better than the alternative. All Swanson needed to do now was get in contact with one of the remaining Escobar brothers. They normally worked in groups of four. There were only three bodies in the house, and if one of them were David, that meant there were two people still outstanding. His guess was Lucas and Diego. They were the more ruthless ones. However, neither of them had responded since the last text message that confirmed that there were issues with the job, which could mean two things; either the surviving members were severely hurt and were resting up somewhere, or they were plotting against Swanson for the death of their brothers. The latter seemed more likely.

The thought sent a chill down his spine. Because if his hunch was spot-on, he was going to have an even bigger issue on his hands. If there was one thing Swanson knew, it was that you did not go to war with the Escobar brothers. They were known for their ruthlessness and were a feared name among the criminal underworld. They were not the kind of people you wanted coming after you.

Swanson hoped this was just his paranoia talking again, but just in case, he was going to have to prepare for the worst. Because if he wanted to see this thing all the way through, and end up on the living side of it, he was going to need some help. And he knew just where he might be able to get it.

36 Chambers

Artur Suites stood fifty-eight stories high. A tower among the city pointing towards the heavens. A gateway for souls that have come and gone. The man could smell the death that lingered on the building's walls and blew into the wind. He wondered how many people had been brought here to be sacrificed to the rich. For their needs, as an offering of suffering.

The man sat inside the lobby, marveling at the design of the hotel, which was immaculate. The man had been in some nice places, but nothing like this. It had a spiral staircase with crystal chandeliers. White walls and lush carpeting. Paintings of old men in suits hanging on the walls. An indoor pool and an upscale restaurant. He wondered if Mr. Vasiliev would be in the master suite tonight. His intel said he would. Maybe he would pay him and his wife a visit once he was done.

The information the man gathered from Amy's laptop told him everything he needed to know about Artur's underground business. Artur had made it so only the initiated could gain access into the playpens via a swipe card. In order to get down into the torture farm, the man needed to get to the service elevator that led down into the play area. It was located at the basement level of the hotel and was always guarded by two armed men. But before he could think about that, the man needed to get an ID card, which shouldn't have been too much of a problem.

The man had a list of names of all the people who were a part of Artur's little club. Most of them had suites at the hotel. All the man had to do was pick a name from the list and find them and relieve them of their property. It was easier done than said.

When the man saw one of the adopters walking through the lobby, he followed him up to his room. Forced him inside. Then snapped his neck. The man took his key card, then walked out with his prize and headed down towards the basement. He opened his lockbox and ran his hand along his white mask. He could hear it calling to him, wanting him. He closed his eyes and slowly placed it on. He was ready. The man walked up towards the guards who gave him an apprehensive look as he approached. One of the guards chuckled.

"We're getting all kinds of freaks coming in here now," the guard said.

"Yeah, but it's always the weirdos who spend the most money. I bet this one is loaded," the other guard stated. He looked at the man who stared back at him through the eyes of his mask. "You're a little early for Halloween."

"Are there armed guards throughout this whole place?" the man asked, his voice was muffled under the mask.

The guards laughed. "Why? Guns make you nervous?" one teased.

"No. I was just curious. The intel I received didn't tell me much about who was stationed on the inside. Just want to make an assessment before I go down."

"This your first time?"

"Here? Yes."

"Don't worry. We only keep security outside the doors. We don't watch and we can't even hear you; everything is soundproof."

"Excellent!" the man said. "You have been much help. Thank you."

The man reached into his coat, grabbed his silencer, and shot both guards in the head. They barely had time to flinch, let alone register the movement of his arm. The man then pulled out the swipe card he was generously given and placed it on the keypad. The elevator door opened up. It took him down into the lounge area of the fun house.

The man could smell the stench of old blood in there. He took the aroma in, savoring it into his lungs as he stepped out into the room, which was all red. Even the bar was the color of blood. There was a monitor in a corner with views of the different chambers where people were being held and played with. One shot showed two men and a woman in business-friendly attire.

Clients.

There were people stationed at the bar; some were sitting in velvet seats, some were standing up, all of them laughing and talking until the man stepped into the room. Now they were just staring at him with judging eyes, eyes that tried to comprehend what the man was, his mask, and its smiling face that stared back at them with contempt.

It demanded blood.

The man reached into his waistband and pulled out a black handgun with a silencer. Their faces switched from judgement to shock to pleading. He shot the three people sitting down in the head, and then the other three who were standing up in the chest. The shots came one after another in quick bursts, the sound little more than a puff of air.

The bartender stood frozen, unsure of what to do. The man looked up towards the monitor. He stood there for a moment just watching the screens. And then, without taking his eyes away from the monitor, he casually raised his gun and shot the bartender three times in the chest. The man then walked over towards the door. He reached onto his belt and pulled off two smoke grenades. He placed the swipe card onto the key pad. The light above the door turned green. He released the grenades as the door opened, then stepped out into the hallway and into the cover of smoke.

His mask and black suit were barely visible as the fog consumed him. Under the mask, his smile almost matched his disguise. He thought about what was to come. He thought about the screams that were about to go unheard to the outside world. He thought about how enjoyable the rest of his evening was going to be. He was going to paint the floors red with blood, and hang the bodies up for decoration. And when he was done here, he would go and do the same to Moretti's strip club. Misery was going to have more than enough company tonight.

Graveyard Shift

It was early in the morning when Swanson went over to Moretti's strip club. He needed to speak to the little man, he needed to see how they could fix the mess Moretti made. Swanson tried calling Moretti but none of his calls were answered. His mind raced as panic swarmed over his thoughts. He'd wondered if Artur had already made his move on Moretti, or if the small man decided to skip town. It wouldn't have surprised Swanson if he had. It actually didn't sound like a bad move; it was one Swanson was considering himself. The thought of getting away, starting over, almost eased his thoughts. Almost. That was, until he pulled up to the parking lot.

There were a bunch of bodies lying on the ground near the entrance of the club. Most of them were security guards, some of them were off-duty police officers. All of them were dead.

Swanson walked around towards the back entrance, the door was hanging open. A bouncer sat slumped in the hallway. His throat was slit. Other bodies were similarly positioned. Swanson carefully stepped over them as he headed towards Moretti's office. Inside were more dead guards.

Blood was splattered on the walls and in pools on the floor. Swanson examined the bodies, one by one. None of them were Moretti. His cellphone started to buzz in his pocket. He grabbed it and glanced at the ID; the caller was Hurst, another detective on the force and also, another person on Artur's payroll.

"Swanson," he answered; the disgust in his voice was apparent as he spoke into the phone. His eyes scanned over the newly-made graveyard.

"Hey, you okay? You sound like you seen a ghost." Hurst said catching Swanson's off tone.

"No. I'm not okay," Swanson said, still taking in the bloody mess.

"Well, I hate to further ruin your day with bad news, but I think you better get over to the Suites."

"I'm off today, Hurst."

"I know you are. But we uh, have a bit of a situation."

The sound in Hurst's voice made Swanson's heart stop. His stomach twisted in knots. He couldn't deal with more bad news. Not right now.

"What kind of fucking situation, Hurst?"

"A bad one. A gonna-make-the-news kind of situation. I think you should just get here and see for yourself before it turns into a circus."

"Okay. All right. Just…give me a few minutes."

Swanson hung up and looked over the scene again. He thought about calling it in, but then changed his mind. He needed to get to the Suites. His mind raced with thoughts. He knew this had to be done by one of two groups of people: the Escobar brothers, who had still not gotten back to Swanson, or Artur Vasiliev, who Swanson hadn't gotten back to. His gut was telling him it was the Escobar brothers. And if that was so, it was going to be an issue, but one that he would have to worry about later. Right now, he needed to try to clean up whatever went down at the Suites. And more importantly, he needed to make sure nothing could get traced back to him.

He rushed over towards the hotel, burdened with a sense of dread. Mainly because he was driving right towards where he knew Artur would be. And that's when the paranoia started to push its way back into the forefront of his mind. What if this was a setup? What if Artur and his men were just waiting for him when he got there? No. Hurst was one of his best men, and he trusted him. If he called for him, then whatever was going on was serious.

Swanson came around the backway and pulled into the hotel's parking garage. Hurst met him at the entrance. He had a "we messed up" look on his face, like a child who couldn't hide their guilt. Hurst was accompanied by two hotel employees. They escorted them to the service elevator, which was covered in blood. Two bodies sat inside of it. Someone had carved permanent smiles on their faces.

"A client saw the bodies and panicked. The hotel called me and, well…here we are," Hurst said as he looked at Swanson. He had an expression on his face that suggested he was hoping Swanson would have a solution for this mess.

Unfortunately, Swanson didn't. He looked just as lost and distraught as his partner. Swanson wiped his face with the palm of his hand and glared over towards the hotel attendants.

"Tell me what the fuck happened."

The attendant shifted uneasily. "I don't know."

"You don't know?"

"No. We, uh, tried to get the security footage, but someone already erased it. Most of it, anyway. The only thing we have is footage of a man in a mask talking to the two people in the elevator. It goes black after that."

Swanson's face filled with raw anger. His skin turned red as his blood boiled.

"You mean to tell me that one guy," Swanson said, holding up his finger, "one,—came in here and just started killing people?"

"Well…everyone except the adopted," the attendant said shakily.

"Excuse me?" Swanson said, stepping closer to the man. His hands were on his hips. His mouth curled up into a scowl. That was not what Swanson wanted to hear.

"Like I said," Hurst cut in. "We have a bit of a problem."

"This whole thing is a fucking problem," Swanson snapped.

He knew this was it for him. He could see it now, his face plastered all over national news. The adopted were a bunch of people from various backgrounds. Some were from Moretti's club. Some were foreigners here in the States illegally. Some were underaged kids. Runaways. Some were just regular people who had the unfortunate luck to be picked out of a hat. Their being alive meant trouble for Swanson. Some of them knew his face because he'd helped escort them in. And if they were as vengeful as he was, they wouldn't hesitate to take the first opportunity to see him burn. Swanson wiped his face with the palm of his hands and exhaled slowly.

"How long before our people get here?"

"I don't think anyone knows yet. I've been trying to keep this contained. Which is why I called you."

"Okay. We need to go down there and—"

"No," Hurst said, shaking his head. "You don't want to go down there."

"Why not?"

"It's a blood bath."

"I've seen blood baths."

"No. Not like this. There are bodies strung up on the walls and hanging from the ceiling like Christmas decorations. I've never seen anything like it. This guy didn't just go in there and kill people. He started setting them up."

"Setting them up?" Swanson asked curiously.

"Yeah, like he was putting up a fucking art exhibit. There's a group of people in the break room with their eyes cut out. He propped them up at a table. Made it look like they were playing a game of cards. He cut into their faces to make it look like they were smiling. He propped another guy up at the edge of his bed. He was holding his detached genitalia in his hands. And those aren't even the worst of it. Trust me."

Swanson scrunched up his face. "What about Artur? Does he know? Is he here?"

Hurst looked at the attendant, then back towards Swanson. His eyes hung open, like he was scared to speak. Swanson didn't care for the suspense.

"What?"

"Artur's dead," Hurst said in a small voice.

This wasn't necessarily bad news for Swanson, but the sound of it still sent a wave of shock through him.

"Excuse me? He's what?"

"Dead. Artur and his wife were found by his son in the

bathroom this morning. Artur was tied to a chair, facing the bathtub. He had his eyelids cut off and his throat slit. His mom was found naked, face down in the water. She had lacerations all over her body. I didn't go up there and see. But Artur's son said her face was pretty much peeled off."

"Jesus!"

"Yeah. And there's, uh, one other thing."

Swanson shook his head. He couldn't take any more "things." Hurst reached into his pocket. He pulled out a plastic baggie. It had a bloody, folded piece of paper inside of it. Swanson examined it, pinching it at the corners.

"Evidence?"

"Possibly. We found it on one of the bodies in the elevator. It was already in the bag when I nabbed it."

The baggie had blood over it. On the outside of the folded letter was Swanson's name. He pulled it out and read the letter silently to himself.

Hello Detective Swanson,

I am sorry to say that you and I will not be meeting face to face anytime soon. Maybe not at all. I've realized that my inactivity over these years has made me a bit careless. But you will be glad to hear that I am finding my way again.

Unfortunately, that means I will have to be leaving soon. I left too many breadcrumbs for me to stick around. I hope this does not disappoint you as much as it does me. But I do not leave you without a parting gift. See, I was scratching my head trying to figure out the best way for me to hurt you. And then it came to me. Like a brisk of wind on a hot day.

I remembered the laptop you and your late boss have been so eagerly wanting to retrieve. To erase all those bad little truths that sit on it. Artur, as you probably know by now, won't be needing it anymore. And I'm certainly not just going to give it to you. But I did send it to one of your colleagues, Ms. Angela.

And if I'm a betting man, Detective Swanson, then I'm sure she has already gone through it and implicated you in more than enough crimes to send you to jail for the rest of your life. Not a fitting end for someone with your status, but one that is ironically poetic. I just know how much cops love jail and putting people in them. I'm sure you have an abundance of friends waiting for you inside. Oh, and don't worry about Mr. Moretti. He's in good hands now. Best of wishes.

From your friend.

There was something more at the bottom of the letter—a disfigured smiley face drawn in blood. The smile was crooked. Its lips curled up at the corners. Swanson crumpled up the paper, his face scrunched into a snarl.

"Fuck! FUCK!" Swanson growled.

"What did the note say?" Hurst asked.

"It said I need to leave."

"Leave?! What about this?" Hurst said gesturing towards the elevator.

"Have the hotel call it in. Let Homicide come and run their investigation. If possible, go downstairs before more officials get here and try and get rid of some of those ears and eyes down there."

"What about you?"

"I have to go."

"Go where? We're going to need you on this one," Hurst insisted. "At the very least, Artur's son is going to want to speak to you about all of this. He's going to have questions. He already said to have you to check in with him."

Swanson shrugged his shoulders. Almost as if he didn't care. "If he has questions, then you can answer them."

"And tell him what?"

"I don't know. Give him the same story you'll be giving the D.A. when they question you. Tell him I'm not here. That you never saw me, that I disappeared."

"I don't think he's going to like that. You and I both know that won't go over well." Swanson thought about that for a moment. In truth, Hurst was right. Dmitri, Artur's son, was surely devastated about the murder of his parents. But he was going to be even more upset when he found out that Swanson left. Dmitri was a violent man, and one who had very little patience for excuses. He wouldn't care why Swanson couldn't prevent his father's death, he would simply just blame him for it. Swanson had witnessed Dmitri's wrath and he did not want to be around for it.

"He'll get over it."

A Meeting with the Devil

Swanson rushed out of the hotel and towards his home. He heard the emergency responders rushing towards the scene, their sirens blaring through the streets like a cry of thunder. He needed to hurry. He wasn't sure how much time he had before his own department came looking for him. His best bet was to just grab what he could and leave. He'd go someplace quiet, exotic, someplace he could be forgotten.

He didn't want to be around while the investigation was taking place. The last thing he wanted was for one of his colleagues to have easy access to him for questioning. He also didn't want to be looking over his shoulder for the rest of his life. Freedom wasn't freedom if you spent it running away. But then again, he'd much rather live free running than to live the rest of his life behind bars.

As he drove up to his street, he saw a black SUV turn the corner. He wondered how long it had followed him, if it indeed was following him. Maybe it was just his paranoia again. He watched it closely, looking more at it than the road ahead. Swanson's house was pretty much secluded, covered by trees. His nearest neighbor was a couple of miles away. This always put him on edge, ironic as it was. He liked his privacy, but today, it was this privacy that might get him killed.

The person behind him made no attempts at turning. Swanson placed his hand on his gun as he neared his driveway, but realized too late that he was trapped. The road ahead was blocked by two more black SUVs and a line of men in black suits. They had their arms crossed in front of them. The SUV behind Swanson came to a stop just as Swanson stopped his own vehicle.

Swanson kept his foot on the gas.

He pondered his next move.

His brain ran through scenarios, options. None of them had good outcomes for him.

A man stepped out of the SUV, and as he walked up towards the car, Swanson's thoughts centered on one option: putting his gun to his head, and pulling the trigger. That had to be better than the alternative. His hand trembled around the gun. He pondered the thought harder and harder, then decided. He couldn't do it. Swanson knew who these guys were. Artur Vasiliev's men. Or at least they used to be. Now they worked for Artur's son. Maybe he could talk his way out of this. He technically hadn't done anything wrong. He didn't kill Artur, and he wasn't the one who attacked the hotel. But as those thoughts crossed Swanson's mind, there were a couple other thoughts that countered them.

Swanson hadn't killed Artur, but he also failed to save him. He failed to find the computer, and failed by allowing this whole situation to escalate to this point. His purpose was gone, and now he was nothing more than a liability.

There was a knock at the window. The person motioned for him to roll it down. It wasn't until now that Swanson noticed it was raining. His thoughts were scattered. His heart sank down deep into the bowels of his stomach. He tasted the last bits of air that surrounded his space, fresh and surprisingly comforting. He took in his last seconds of feeling nothing, and cherished that feeling. Because soon, his world was going to be filled with agonizing pain. Karma had a funny way of showing itself; its lessons, as Swanson now knew, were cruel. Swanson rolled down his window. His eyes stayed focused on the men in front of him.

"Artur's son would like to speak to you, detective. Would you mind stepping out of the car and coming with me? I will escort you to him."

Swanson nodded slowly, his face a beaten scowl. He scratched his nose and unbuckled his seatbelt. His hand eased off his gun.

"Don't worry about your car, detective. One of our guys will take care of it."

A Bad Place To Wake Up

Moretti's eyes opened slowly. He heard opera music playing in the background. Faint under the buzzing in his head. His vision was blurry, the area around him distorted. His body felt heavy, restricted. His throat was dry. He blinked repeatedly to try to help his vision come in a little better. When it did, he was greeted to a naked body hanging from the ceiling, its head slumped down. Dry blood crusted its limbs. Its stomach was cut open, leaving its insides dangling out and splattering onto the floor before him. The stench was sour, like old garbage mixed with spoiled meat. Moretti started to dry heave.

"Jesus Christ!" he screamed out. He tried to pull his arms free, but they were tied tightly to the chair he was positioned in. He jerked his feet up and screamed as pain flared up his ankles and legs. He looked down and saw that his feet had been nailed to the floor beneath him. "Jesus CHRIST!" he screamed again. "Where am I? WHERE AM I?"

"Nowhere Jesus would be," a voice said from the far side of the room.

Moretti turned his head to the sound of the voice. A man sat in a chair in front of a desk. The shadows hovered over him and around the light from the computer screen he was looking at.

"What is this?!" Moretti screamed.

The man didn't respond and kept clicking away at his keyboard. Moretti didn't look at the body in front of him. He didn't want to. He tried to keep his eyes on the man. And as he did, he realized that he recognized him. His bald head. His glasses. His casual clothing.

"You're that guy. The one that came into the club looking for Amy, right?" He looked further over onto the man's desk. There was a mask there, heavily covered in blood. "You're the guy that's been hunting us."

The man sat back in his chair. He cracked his neck then stood up. He turned around and started to move over to Moretti, walking slowly as he took off his glasses. He cleaned them off with his shirt and placed them on Moretti's face, who flinched as the man's hands came up.

"It's okay," the man comforted. "Open your eyes," he said in a soft voice.

Moretti did, slowly. He was shocked that he was actually able to see clearly through the glasses the man placed on him. The man stood in front of him, studying Moretti's expression. He leaned down until he was face to face with his subject.

"What do you see when you look at me?" the man asked. He glared directly into Moretti's eyes. There was something unsettling about the man, something wrong with the closeness of his presence. He could feel him breathing and it made him horribly uncomfortable.

"A man," Moretti said with a tone that held bits of fear in it.

The man shook his head. "No," he said in a whisper. "Your end."

Moretti stiffened.

"I will be the last person on this earth you will ever get to spend time with," the man continued. He stood up straight. "Would you like some water before we start?"

"Fuck you and your water!" Moretti snapped.

"That language is not nice, Mr. Moretti."

"Do you know who I am? What I know? I can be a very valuable to you. I know things. I have information that—"

The man shook his head. "You mean the information you gave Amy?" the man said, leaning back onto a metal table. "Mr. Moretti, I need you to understand something. You are not here because of the information you have. You're here because of the information I already have. Knowing this might help you going forward. I would hate for you to waste your last breaths on trying to make deals."

Moretti shook his head from side to side. His forehead was sweating. He was breathing hard. His heartbeat was pumping fast as it overworked. His body was anticipating the pain to come.

"Detective Swanson. Artur Vasiliev. You kill me and, trust me, one or both of them will hunt you down like a dog! There won't be an inch of this earth you will be able to walk on without looking over your shoulder. I promise you that," Moretti threatened.

The man walked over to the hanging cadaver and pulled a knife from its torso.

"I don't think so, Mr. Moretti," he said, glancing over at his playmate from the corner of his eyes. "Mr. Vasiliev won't be bothering anyone else. And I'm sure this will be very upsetting to his son. So much so that he won't have an ounce of care left in him to consider your whereabouts. It will also most certainly upset him that Swanson didn't live up to the expectations of protection Swanson and his men were supposed to give. I do believe that by now Swanson, if he hasn't been arrested, has been erased. Or, like you say, he will be too busy looking over his shoulder to worry about you. And on the off chance that he isn't, well, that won't matter. Because he won't have any need to look for me."

The man raised the knife and looked at his reflection. The blood on it distorted the image of his face. He stood there for a moment looking at it, taking himself in. Taking everything in. His new life had burned away and his old one had reared its head back into his world. He was foolish to think he could be anything other than who he was meant to be. He had denied himself true happiness for far too long.

After a while of staring into the knife, there was a twitch on the man's face. A subtle one at the corner of his lip. His face started to strain, like it had just figured out how to express itself. Like it was molding. He felt something coming. He felt himself transforming. His mouth became a grin that his face worked hard to make, as it strained to form into itself. The pieces of his mask fell off completely. His muscles worked hard, ripping and tearing as his face became something familiar, he had found his smile. A real one. One he had thought he lost. Moretti was sickened by it. Frightened. It wasn't a comforting smile. Or one that gave off any remote resemblance to happiness. It looked tortured and ragged. A grin from hell.

"There you are," the man said softly to his reflection. He turned to Moretti, but not as the man he was before. The man had become himself. His old self. His eyes were filled with murderous glee. They stared directly into Moretti's eyes. He pierced through them like he was looking into the depths of Moretti's soul, like he yearned for it. He started to move closer, and as he did, his smile made him look a little more unhinged.

The man stood over Moretti, outlining the skin on his toy's face with the tip of his knife. He brought it down the length of Moretti's torso and spoke with a voice that sounded like it came from the depths of an endless darkness.

"Are you ready for us to begin, Mr. Moretti?"

Epilogue

Kristen heard about David's death. Everyone in the town did. It was all over the news. She felt somewhat responsible for it. She had told those men where David lived, and that was something she would have to live with. She saw how they looked. She knew they were up to no good. But she was mad. She wanted David to hurt for what he said about her. She wanted him to feel as helpless as he had made her feel, and those men looked more than capable of making that happen. But now, she wished more than anything that she could take it back. But she knew that was never going to happen.

Following David's death, things had gotten weird around town. There was a series of gruesome murders, one that police officials had connected to a gang war. High-ranking officials in the police force, as well as business owners around town, were brought up on charges ranging from murder, to kidnapping, to torture, and even rape. Never did she think something like that could happen in her town. And it didn't end there. Currently, there was an attempt to locate a missing police detective. Kristen didn't know what to think of that.

She quit her job at the market and went to work as a waitress. She couldn't stand being at Shop Smart anymore, not after everything that happened. The hours were late, but it paid better than the market. The worst part for her was walking home. The night always seemed so lonely, with the wind being the only thing keeping her company, along with the stars that blinked down from the heavens. And tonight felt like the worst of it.

There was nothing outside, not even the wind. Just the blanket of the night that covered the city. And as lonely as the street she walked on was, she didn't feel alone. It wasn't a comforting feeling. It felt more like a threat, like danger was following behind her lurking in the corners.

As Kristen walked home, she thought she heard someone following her. She turned around to see nothing but the trees and cars that lined the street. Maybe her mind was making up the noise; it had to be.

She continued forward and heard it again. The soft click of footsteps as they clashed with the asphalt. She stopped and turned around. Nothing. She started walking faster. The footsteps behind her matched her pace, becoming louder as if someone wanted her to hear them. She turned around again. Nothing.

"I have a gun and pepper spray!" she screamed. There was no one there, nothing but the night and its shadows. She was about a block away from her home when she decided to sprint the rest of the way there. She fumbled with her keys when she got to her door, nearly dropping them. She opened it hurriedly and slammed it shut, locking it as she entered into her dark home. It caught her off guard; her mother always kept the lights on for her so she didn't have to walk through a dark house at night.

"Mom, I'm home," she said, to no response. She couldn't see ahead of her. She could barely make out the outlines of the room. "Mom?" she questioned. Still nothing. Her heart was racing. Partially because she just got done running for her life and partially because she was horribly afraid of the dark. She had her father to thank for that.

She thought she felt something touch the back of her neck as she walked into the shadowy living room. She hurried across, racing like the floor was filling with lava. She ran towards the light switch, knocking into something as she did, almost tripping over her feet. She hit the switch and gasped as she stared at her living room, which was decorated with pictures.

There were photos of her when she was younger. Photos of her and her father. Her hands clasped over her mouth. Tears started to roll down her face. On the walls hanging from strings on the ceiling were more pictures, all of them greeting her like a sick blast from the past, coming full force and smashing directly into her present, smiling and laughing at her progress of forgetting her trauma. Of changing her life.

Photos of her when she was fat.

Photos of her in her dance recital uniform with her father kneeling down next to her.

And one too many photos of her sitting on his lap with a somber expression.

She started ripping them off of the walls, pulling them from the ceiling, screaming as she tore them to pieces. It wasn't until she started turning towards the kitchen that she saw an outline of a body, standing still in the corner. She shrieked, and when she did, the power in the house went out. She stood still for a moment, frozen, as she kept her eyes on the corner of the room. The figure's face started to light up, its mask glowing in the dark, looking at her with its devilish grin.

Her breaths became shallow, her body tensed.

She felt her legs wobble.

Adrenaline pumped through her. Fight or flight took over. She shook her head as she back-stepped away. Her head turned towards the kitchen. The power box was in the basement. She didn't want to walk past the figure. She didn't want to walk through the house in the dark. So instead, she went with her only option.

She started to move back towards the front door, her eyes focused on the glowing, smiling face from hell. Her hands shook as they reached into her purse. She grabbed her phone and dropped it. She tried to catch it before it hit the floor, but her fingers knocked into it. It flipped in the air then crashed onto the floor.

She bent down and accidently kicked it with her foot. She felt around the floor blindly, trying her best to keep her eyes on the thing in the corner. She felt her lungs clamp up. She was holding her breath. She breathed out between sobs. She looked back up and scanned the darkness. Her fingers pressed against her phone, she blindly grabbed it.

She stood up and started to dial 911. She stepped back carefully, then stopped as her body slammed against something. Something that felt like a person.

She stopped cold just as she was about to hit the call button. Her finger froze over it. She swallowed hard. She could hear someone breathing behind her. She felt the heat of the person's breath on her neck.

The person leaned in close, pressing their body against hers and felt gently down the length of her arm. Their fingertips were rough and calloused. The person reached out and took her phone out of her hands. A knife rested on her opposite shoulder. She trembled as she cried. Urine ran down her leg. And then the person spoke with a soft comforting voice.

A whisper in her ear.

"Hello, Kristen," the man said. "Would you like me to tell you why you cut now?"